Jim Long

HOMECOMING

Jim Long: Homecoming
By Ronnie Ashmore

Published by Creative Texts Publishers, LLC
PO Box 50
Barto, PA 19504
www.creativetexts.com

ISBN: 978-1-64738-077-9

Jim Long

HOMECOMING

by

RONNIE ASHMORE

For Deanna and Melissa.

Growing up with you guys was a blast.

I Love You Both More Than Words Can Say.

CONTENTS

PART I

1

"He's 'round here somewhere. Find him and kill 'im."

The man heard the words but couldn't understand why they were talking about him. The speaker was a tall, wiry dark-haired stranger the man did not recognize as he had no enemies here that he could recall.

He kept low and out of sight. Daring not to move from his hiding spot. He would be hard to see in the dark, hidden as he was in the brush of a big cedar tree that stood beside the cabin. The man had no idea how many there were.

He had heard the riders coming up the lane to the cabin. It was late for visitors, already full dark. Besides, he had no cause to have visitors at any hour, much less this late.

He extinguished the lamp that was on the table when he'd heard the horses coming.

Stepping into the dark and moving from in front of the cabin, he was just lucky to have stepped toward the cedar tree, since the other side of the cabin was exposed.

When he heard the unforgettable snick-snick sound of a rifle being levered, he took cover under that big cedar tree.

He laid flat on the ground and listened to the riders

circle the cabin. It was a small cabin, barely big enough for him. They took so much time looking it over and searching it, you would have thought it was a mansion. When they were done searching, they gathered back outside around the dark-haired leader.

"He ain't nowhere 'round here. Maybe he done runned off," an older man said.

"I doubt it," the leader responded, "but we can make it where he don't run back here."

The leader went inside for a moment. He came out carrying the lamp from inside. He handed it to another man.

"Lamp is still warm. He's somewhere abouts. We won't find him now, though. Will, light this place up."

"What?" The man named Will asked.

He was a younger man barely out of his teens or so it seemed to the stranger as he watched from his cover. Of all the men, he seemed the most reluctant to be there.

"Burn it down," the leader said, mounting his horse.

The others, there were six horses in all, followed suit. Will took a match from his pocket and lit the lamp. The man watched helplessly as Will tossed it into the cabin. The flames caught and the cabin began burning.

The one named Will mounted beside the leader. They all turned and rode away.

The man waited, watching until they were down the

lane about fifty yards, then crawled out of the cedar brush.

He needed to get his guns from inside the now fully burning cabin.

Fighting through smoke and flame, he retrieved his rifle and his pistol. Coughing, and eyes burning, with flames spreading fast and hot, he dragged his smoldering saddle out of the cabin.

All along, one thought kept running through his mind.

Who were they, and why would they want him dead?

2

Dawn came slowly the next morning. He had sat the rest of the night on the ground watching the flames destroy the cabin and burn itself out.

As he thought of who could have done this and came up empty. Nobody he knew would want to kill him.

He was raised in these parts but left home when he was just shy of his fourteenth birthday. A drifter by nature, he had been a traveling man his whole life since. He had originally taken off out west before the war because his ma was afraid that he'd be conscripted into a fight he had no business being in. That war had ended five years ago.

He grew up poor, too poor to have any slaves, or know anyone with slaves. Also, his family had no interest in whether Texas was in the union or not. They were too busy trying to survive.

He had traveled a lot, out to California, spending time in the territories out west. He did some mining, cowboying, and even served a stretch as a deputy in Colorado Territory.

Recently, he had decided he was coming home to Texas, to the place he was born.

That's how he ended up here in this parcel of a shack by the Leon River. The old homeplace was lost to memory, he could not recall where it had been exactly. But he had found this abandoned cabin about a month ago and began fixing it up.

He'd had no visitors nor seen anyone since being back. It had been a solitary life and he loved it. So, he had no idea who Will was or why he and his friends would want to kill him. But he intended to find out.

As he saddled his horse, he noticed the charred edges of the saddle by the cinch strap. He felt the burnt spots with his finger and felt anger rising in him.

He always considered himself a peaceful man, believing in live and let live. But the visitors from the night before obviously didn't subscribe to that notion. He wanted to know why.

He finished saddling the horse, then checked his guns. His Henry rifle appeared to be in working order and the Colt worked like it should. Stepping into the saddle, he headed for town.

The ride into town gave him time to think. It might not be a good idea to tell his business to just anyone until he knew if he could trust anyone.

He had never been to this town they called Leonville, but he imagined it was like a lot of towns that were springing up on the frontier.

He rode into town around eight in the morning, he decided he would get a hotel room since he had no cabin now. Maybe by staying in town he would get that much closer to knowing who the night visitors were.

Leonville was bigger than expected and looked prosperous for a little village. There were all kinds of shops and stores lining the main street. His only interest was in the livery at the moment.

He was dismounting as an old man came walking out from inside the barn.

"Care for my horse awhile?"

He spit a stream of tobacco juice, some getting on his shirt, "Sure. Dollar a week."

He paid him for a week's stay, then walked to the hotel wanting to get the room taken care of. He kept a lookout for any of the night visitors even though he didn't think he would recognize any of them. His next thought gave him a start, he nearly stopped in his tracks. What if his visitors knew him by sight?

He looked the town over better as he walked. It was a neat little settlement not unlike others he had seen. The general store sat in the middle of the main street with the dry goods store across the street. The blacksmith and livery were side by side with one another.

He took another look at the various shops, probably twelve in all. He continued to the hotel.

3

Sitting in his room staring out the window watching the town folk, he felt like a fool. What if the men who had burned him out knew who he was? They would recognize him before he could even know them.

He had signed the hotel registry with a fake name when he had checked in, surely Abraham Lincoln wouldn't mind much. The clerk didn't seem to pay any attention to him as he'd written it down.

He got up and stretched, putting his gun belt on. He wanted to go to the saloon, if there was to be trouble, he would just as soon have it now than later. if there was none, then he could look for answers.

The saloon was empty when he walked in, just the bartender who was cleaning and setting up. He was a skinny man with a light mustache. He looked up as Long stopped in front of the bar.

"Beer," he said, though he wasn't much of a drinking man, especially at one in the afternoon.

The bartender sat the glass in front of him and he put two bits on the bar.

The saloon was a narrow single room affair with just a few tables. No poker tables in sight. No upstairs for adult entertainment, either.

"Nice town."

He looked at the stranger, "You passin' through?"

"May stay. if I find the right place along the river."

"It is a nice town. River country is a little rough from what I hear tell."

A saloon was the best place to hear the latest news. It was the same in all saloons in the west. He was hoping this bartender was in the giving mood when it came to information.

"How's that?"

"Not for me to say, stranger."

He moved off down the bar, suddenly busy wiping a spot at the far end. Long took a seat at a table and sipped his beer slowly.

He was unfamiliar with this town and its workings, but he had seen towns like this before. Someone would think they were a town tough and would want to know who the stranger was.

He sat there for an hour drinking his one beer. He kept looking out the window at the people. The street was bustling with activity. Men and women going about their daily business not worried about strange visitors in the night trying to burn them out and kill them.

He looked over at the bartender who was still wiping

the bar and cleaning up.

"Who's the local law here?"

He looked up at Long for a moment, who thought he wasn't going to answer, then he said,

"What you need with a lawman?"

"Maybe I need to report a crime or something. What does that matter?"

He shrugged a shoulder and laid the rag aside.

"Matters only that we do have a marshal in the common sense meaning of the word. Sure, we have someone with that title, but I wouldn't go counting on him for nothing."

"What does that mean? What's the criminal element like in this little town?"

The bartender picked up the rag again and started wiping the bar. Long stood from his chair and walked up to the bar. He grabbed the rag from the bartender's hand and tossed it to the other end of the bar. He leaned in close.

"Mister, I am getting tired of talking in circles. Give me some straight answers before I lose my temper."

Long was not a small man; he stood a bit over six feet and weighed around two hundred pounds and knew that he could be an intimidating force when need be. The bartender was starting to believe it.

"Just that we don't need much law here. Mr. Ritter takes care of the criminals and drifters who come through here. Tittle don't need to do much."

He eased back a little, moving away from the bar. he walked to the end where he had thrown the rag and picked it up. he handed it to the bartender and said,

"Who's Ritter?"

The bartender accepted the towel, watching Long.

"You will probably meet him sooner than you want to. He probably already knows you're here. I wouldn't be surprised if one of his men isn't searching your hotel room right now."

Long hesitated only a moment, he took off out of the saloon and made a fast walk to his hotel room. After the events of the last night, the thought of someone going through what little he had left rankled him something fierce.

4

As Long entered the hotel and made his way upstairs to his room, he saw a man coming out of the room. The stranger closed the door gently, then turned to walk down the hall toward Long.

As he came closer, he glanced up at Long and nodded. Long, without hesitation, hit him square in the face. Hard.

The blow busted the man's nose, spraying blood over his face. Long hit him a second time in the stomach taking his wind from him. Long heard the air leaving his lungs.

Grabbing him by the collar of his shirt, he half dragged the intruder back to his room. Once inside the room, Long sat him in the lone straight back chair and hit him in the face again, knocking the chair back sending both man and chair crashing to the floor.

Long picked the chair up and set it right, then sat the man back in the chair. Long took the man's pistol from his holster and put it behind his own waistband.

The man was bleeding, and one eye was starting to swell.

"I'm gonna ask some questions and each time you lie or don't answer I'm gonna hit you. Understand?"

"You goin' to tie me up and threaten me?"

HOMECOMING

"Not tie you up. I want your hands free so if you decide you want to fight back, I can just kill you and it will be a fair fight."

The man looked at his captor through his good eye,

"Kill me? You're crazy. Do you know who I work for?"

"Ritter would be my guess. I don't care who you work for or what Ritter thinks he's doing. You come after me, I come after you. Now, what are you doing in my room?"

The man lowered his head, shook it a moment, then looked back up.

"I'm just following what I was told. Go look at the new guy's room and see who he is."

"So, who am I?"

"There was nothing here to tell me that. Who are you? Mister Ritter will want to know."

"Where do I find Ritter, I'll tell him myself."

The man was silent for a long time. Long hit him again in the face but on the opposite side. His head swung violently with the impact of the punch.

"Don't hit me, okay. Ritter finds you. You don't go to him."

"I should kill you."

"You might as well. You made it where Mr. Ritter will consider me a failure. He don't like failure."

RONNIE ASHMORE

"What's your name?"

"Pendleton."

"Well, Pendleton, here is what you will do. You go to the livery, get your horse, and ride out of here now. Get out of the country. If I see you or if I hear you are still around, I will come kill you wherever you are. Understand?"

He looked at Long confused for a moment.

"You mean ride out?"

"As fast and as far as you can. First, I want an answer. Who is Will?"

"What? Will who?"

"I don't know who, but I am betting you do. Will?"

"He works for Ritter."

"Where do I find Ritter?"

"He has a spread just east of here. It's a large one too. But he will be in town tomorrow for business. I'd wait for him here if you want to talk to him."

"Why?"

"He wants to know who you are. I don't know why but he seemed worried when he heard you were in town."

"All right, Pendleton, get on out of town now. Remember what I said."

Pendleton stood slowly from the chair, watching Long. His face was a bloody mess that would surely attract attention on the street. He walked to the door then looked back.

"My pistol?" he said, nodding at the gun in the other man's waistband.

Long stared at him, then smiled.

"You don't own a pistol anymore."

5

As Long sat in his hotel room, he was staring out the window watching as Pendleton went toward the livery and then left town. This sitting around was getting him nowhere. His thoughts ran wild as he watched the goings on in the street.

He could leave the area. Just ride out and never look back. He dismissed that thought as soon as he had it.

This Leon River area was all he thought of when he had thoughts of home. Though there was never any kin around the area in the old days, so he had no idea whatever happened to his ma or pa. He wrote a few letters but never had a proper place to receive any mail back. When he thought of his folks, he thought of this area of Texas. And he would not run.

He needed to figure out who Ritter was though. And why he wanted him dead. Long knew no one by that name. This town had not been here when he had left out years ago, so it went to reason that Ritter was not here then, either. He needed to do some research, but quietly.

Long had to do something to be able to protect himself from unknown enemies. He was a smooth shot with any firearm. He learned from some great frontiersmen in his travels. He needed to be prepared to shoot at a moment's notice. He probably wouldn't have time to be patient and take aim in a root hog or die shooting. If you don't know when that will be, how do you prepare for something like that?

Long's thinking was you don't. You shoot to kill, and you shoot first. That's the only thing some of these people understand.

What he was having trouble understanding was why this man named Ritter was after him. Long had no idea who he was or why he wanted him dead. But he intended to find out. Somehow.

He went downstairs and noticed the clerk looking at him strangely. he didn't like the look he was receiving, not one bit.

Long stared back at him as he got to the bottom of the stairs.

"You let anyone else in my room, desk clerk, it will be you I come for next. Understand?"

Long kept walking as he stared over at the clerk. He saw that his words had the impact he intended even though the man did not answer back.

Out on the street, he had no idea where he was going. He went to the saloon since it was the only place in town a stranger could go without giving it too much thought.

The barkeeper gave Long a look as he walked in. Long

raised one eyebrow toward the man as he looked around the still empty bar.

"Stranger, you cut quite a path. I will say that," the barman said.

He sat a glass of beer on the bar top. Long laid a coin on the bar and took a long drink of beer. He looked at the bartender and nodded his thanks.

"What's your name?" Long said.

"Silas. I own this saloon."

He refilled Long's glass, refusing the coin he offered him.

"I don't know what else to say to you except Ritter is going to be mad when he finds out Pendleton turned tail and ran. He looked awful when he came for a drink. Said he was clearing out. He didn't want any more to do with the stranger."

Long said nothing, just sipped his beer.

"Most folks don't stay around town long after making Ritter mad."

"How long has this town been here?"

"Few years, it's a decent town for a new town."

"I need directions to Ritter's spread. How can I find him?"

The bartender looked at Long for a long time, then moved down to the end of the bar, ignoring the question.

HOMECOMING

Long was tempted to ask again, but two men came into the saloon and interrupted my plans.

6

Long watched as they came in. They were looking at him, their eyes never leaving Long's. The two moved to a table and sat down. The older looking one was still staring as he sat down. The younger one had already moved on to look at his partner.

They were dressed in rough range clothes that had seen better days, but their guns were taken care of, and they both wore them as if just the presence of them should warn danger away.

Long was having none of it, he grinned at them as he watched them.

"What's wrong gents? You look like you drank some sour buttermilk. Let me buy you a drink, how about it?"

Long didn't know why he said it, but the words had the desired effect. The older one tipped his hat back on his head a little and stared at Long full on.

"Are you making fun, mister?" he said.

"Offering to buy you a drink."

The bartender cleared his throat, then said to the two men,

HOMECOMING

"Listen, Chance, Will, I was just telling this fella here that there was no work around here right now. Not even Mr. Ritter is hiring."

Will? Was this the same Will that had been a part of the group that burned the cabin? Maybe this was a different Will.

The older man stared at Long as he answered the bartender.

"Seems you talk too much, Silas. Just keep pouring drinks and keep your opinion to yourself."

Long decided to poke the bear, so to speak.

"You boys hear of the cabin that was burned down late last night, just out of town?"

That got the young man named Will's attention. He lifted his head to look at Long, then looked over at his friend, Chance.

Silas took the opportunity to try and change the subject.

"How about that drink, gentleman?" he said.

The one called Chance shook his head, then said,

"What do you know about the cabin burning?"

"Me?" Long said, shaking his head. "Nothing. Just what gossip I have heard on the street. Whoever did it caused a stir, though. Nobody knows what happened to the man who lived in the cabin. I heard he was shot while running from the fire."

RONNIE ASHMORE

Both men stood to leave at the same time. Long watched as they walked from the room saying nothing else, then he turned back to the bartender.

"I'm going to need a map to Ritter's place."

7

Long studied the map the bartender had given him. Long had to promise not to tell how he came about having it if he was caught with it.

It was about a five-mile ride to the headquarters of Ritter's spread. He had some time to get there and get back before nightfall.

He didn't want to get caught on the trail after dark. He still had enemies that he didn't know lurking around. He put the map in his pocket and left the saloon, going to the livery.

He got his horse and as he was saddling up, he kept a lookout for anyone who may have been watching too closely.

A half hour later he rode into the yard of the Ritter ranch. Hard stares from the three hands greeted him as he reined up in front of the house.

A man who seemed to carry himself with authority walked up to Long, unsmiling, unfriendly.

"Can I help you?"

"Need to see Mr. Ritter."

The man laughed a short laugh.

"Is that right? Well, not just anyone gets to see Mr. Ritter. What's this about?"

"Are you Ritter? If not, then I'll wait for him here."

The man looked at Long hard. There was hate in his eyes, he was not used to being confronted like he had just been.

"Go on," Long said, not taking his eyes off the man.

The man didn't like it, not one bit. But he went and stepped onto the porch of the main house, which was solidly built from wood beams not available in the area.

Long stayed in the saddle as the hand knocked on the door. When the door was answered, a man of around fifty came out and spoke softly to the hand. He came to the edge of the porch and looked at Long.

"What's the meaning of this?" he said.

"Come to ask a question and deliver a message."

The older man said nothing, so Long waited him out. Ritter looked at his foreman, then back at Long, finally he spoke.

"Well?"

"The question is, Do you know anything about my cabin being burned out last night? Some men in town seemed to think you did."

"I most certainly do not. And I resent the fact you come riding in here demanding answers as if you are entitled."

"Then my statement will really get your hackles up. If I see any of your men around my place as I rebuild, or I feel threatened in any way in town by them. I will come looking for you."

"You piss ant," he said, stepping on the top step of the porch stairs.

His foreman moved toward Long as well, but Long turned his horse blocking the foreman's path and rode out of the yard without another word being said. He felt he had made his point.

But had he? Only time would tell on that. Another thought struck him. What if he was wrong? What if Ritter knew nothing of the attack on the cabin?

The odds seemed to say otherwise. Chance and Will, who were in the saloon earlier, knew of the attack on the cabin. He was sure of that. And they both worked for Ritter. Ritter knew.

8

Long knew he had to be careful. Ritter and his men would be looking to cause trouble at any moment.

But trouble was what he was made for. Seems it was all he had known since his youth. He needed to find out more about Ritter and how big of a loop he swung in this country.

No doubt picking a fight with him was taking on the big rooster of the hen house. But he didn't care. His cabin, as that is how he had come to think of the abandoned cabin he had stumbled upon, was burned to the ground and men wanted to kill him. And for what he did not know.

The law, such as it was, would be no help to a stranger. He never was much dependent on the law handling his problems anyway.

He rode into town cautious. He left his horse at the livery, took his saddlebags, and headed back to his room. He caught the smell of food from the restaurant in town and realized he was hungry.

The few people in the place turned and stared at as he walked in the door. Each person had various looks on their faces, from surprise to pity.

HOMECOMING

He took a seat at a table in the corner. The lady, probably Long's age or younger, approached looking tired and worn out, pad and pencil in hand.

"What's with the welcome committee?" he said.

"You want to order," she said louder than necessary.

He looked at her for a moment, then gave her his order, she made a show of writing it down. As she wrote, she said,

"You best be careful, mister. You made some enemies already."

She moved off to get the food. He glanced at the room from the corner of my eye. The men looking at him had no friendliness in their eyes. The women ignored him for the most part.

The lady came back and set the food down heavily, clanking the silverware on the plate.

"Eat slow."

He was hungry and he wasn't sure he could eat slowly, but he did his best to take his time on the beans and cornbread that tasted better than anything he'd had in a long time.

Eventually the crowd drifted out as they finished eating. He was sopping up beans with a piece of cornbread when the last family left.

RONNIE ASHMORE

The waitress peeked out of the kitchen and looked around. She came to the table holding a coffee pot, but made no attempt to refill the cup.

"You make enemies fast."

"How so?" he said, swallowing his last bite.

"Men are talking about you asking after Mr. Ritter. Said you was gonna ride out to his place."

"Mr. Ritter is something important around here, is he?"

"You keep pushing his men or him and you will find out," she said, watching him closely.

"You don't seem too worried about him. Why is that?"

"That's my business."

She turned and walked away. He sat there feeling out of sorts. He had no idea what he had gotten himself into by taking on Ritter. But he knew it was going to be painful for someone. He just hoped it wasn't him.

Long left the restaurant and went back to the only hotel. He was looking forward to going to the room and going to sleep. As he entered the hotel lobby from the porch, he knew sleep would have to wait.

A man wearing a star on his shirt pocket was waiting, sitting on the sofa, his dirty clothes a contrast to the cleanliness of the lobby.

He stood as Long walked in.

"Need to talk to you for a moment, stranger."

HOMECOMING

Long ignored him, nodded to the clerk, who seemed nervous as he stared from Long to the lawman.

"You hear me, mister?"

Long turned and looked at the lawman a long moment, then said,

"I'm tired. I have no business with you. You want to talk, see me at breakfast in the morning at the restaurant."

Long turned and walked toward the stairs that led to his room. As he reached the top landing, he looked down at the lobby from the corner of his eye. The lawman and the clerk were standing there looking up at the stranger.

9

The next morning Long was at the restaurant before daylight. He was the first customer there. The same young lady was back and took his order. She came back and set a full coffee cup in front of him.

"Anything you can tell me about the law in this town," he said, watching her set the cup down.

She glanced at the clock on the wall.

"You can ask him yourself in about five minutes. He will be here then."

Again, she moved off like she didn't want to bother talking. Maybe she didn't, Long thought, after all he was a drifting saddle bum and not much to look at anyway.

Was a drifting saddle bum, he reminded himself. That was before he came back to his home country to settle down. Before the cabin he had claimed was burned out and people he didn't know tried to kill him. He had no business thinking of women when he was in such a dangerous situation.

Almost to the time, the lawman walked into the restaurant. He looked Long's way, then over to the waitress. He nodded at her, then came to the table. Without an invite he pulled a chair out and sat down.

HOMECOMING

"Do you feel rested enough to talk now?"

Long stared at him, saying nothing. He let the silence linger as the waitress set a cup of coffee in front of the lawman. She looked at Long as if he were dense.

"We can drag this out all day if you want, or you can talk over a nice meal. Your choice," the lawman said.

"OK. Let's talk."

"What's your name?"

"My name don't matter much. It ain't a name you'd know. I'm not wanted anywhere or suspected of anything."

"Why are you in town then?"

"My cabin was burned out. Men tried to kill me. Men I believe work for Ritter."

The lawman sipped his coffee.

"You went to see Ritter," he said.

It wasn't a question, so Long only shrugged.

"What purpose did that serve?"

Long leaned forward, looking the lawman in the eyes.

"My cabin was burned down. I was threatened with death for no reason I can think of. Ritter did that or he ordered it done. I will find out why and I will give payback as needed."

"Ritter ain't much for being pushed around."

"He's never been pushed by me. That payback goes for whoever is helping him too."

"Meaning?"

Long said nothing. He just stared at the lawman and let the words hang in the air. He had no doubt the law was not on the side of who was right but rather on the side of the man who had given him his job.

"I'm eating now, deputy," he said.

The marshal caught the intended insult and stood from the chair.

"It's Marshal. Marshal Tittle. You best keep your nose clean in town, mister. It might get broken."

He stormed out of the restaurant and a few seconds later the lady brought his plate of food from the kitchen. She looked at the empty space where moments ago he had been sitting.

"What happened to the Marshal?"

"Something made his stomach turn sour, I reckon."

She placed the plate on the table, sighed, and wiped her hands on her apron.

"You make a lot of commotion, don't you?" she said.

"I need to know more about this town. You feel like being a history teacher?"

She just stared at him, silently.

10

Long left the restaurant not knowing what to do the rest of the day. The sun was up and it was going to be hot. He needed to explore the town a little more. He was certain he had figured out the power rankings of the little place, but he was a man that needed intel before he made a decision.

As he made his way around town, he became aware that nobody greeted him, nobody smiled when he tried looking friendly, and nobody looked at him straight on. It seemed their attention was always diverted.

Same thing when he would go into a store. No clerk greeted him, no one waited on him, no one asked any questions at all.

Feeling frustrated, he went to the Marshal's Office. As he entered, Tittle looked up from his work at his desk. It was a small office, with a battered desk, a wood stove to his right that was cold now, and a single file cabinet behind the old desk. The rack along one wall that normally would hold rifles was empty. There was a single cell that was along the far wall, it too was empty. All in all, it was a fitting office for a token lawman.

Tittle tossed his paperwork on his desk, as he looked up at Long.

"Well, what brings you in here?"

RONNIE ASHMORE

"Wanted to tell you, this is a right unfriendly town you have here," Long said.

The way Long stood in front of his desk forced Tittle to crane his neck to look up at him.

"Well, they ain't used to strangers kicking up a fuss around here. That's all."

"I guess they are OK with strangers being burned out of their property, though, right?"

"You think that old abandoned cabin was yours? I forget whose it was originally, but I know it wasn't yours."

Tittle stood, looking Long straight in the eyes. He was a little shorter than Long's six foot, but not by much.

"What are you really doing here, mister?"

"Settling down. Was anyway. I was born and raised in this area. I took off out west before the war. This town wasn't here. None of this was here then. My home place is lost to my mind, but I know it was somewhere around here. I aim to stay, and nobody will run me out."

"Raised here, you say. There couldn't have been much in this country then, I guess."

"I remember a few families, the Redding's, the Moore's. Then our family of course."

"Never heard of them. Which reminds me, you never told me your name."

HOMECOMING

"No, I didn't. Until I find out why people want me dead, I'll keep that to myself."

"Well, be that as it may, I have to call you something, don't I?"

Long turned and walked to the door. He opened it to step outside but Tittle's voice stopped him for a moment.

"Don't go looking for trouble, you hear."

Long left the office and stood on the street for a moment trying to gather his thoughts. He had mentioned other families he had known growing up. Were any of them still around? How could he find out if their places still existed if he didn't know for sure where his place had been?

It was something to think about. He could ask around town but everyone seemed closed minded and standoffish. The bartender and the woman at the restaurant were the only ones in town that had shown him any kindness.

Why?

He walked over to the saloon to see if the bartender, Silas, was still there.

As he entered, he saw a man standing at the bar sipping beer. He turned to look at Long as he came in. Long paid him no mind as he walked to the other side of the bar. There were only a few other men he didn't recognize sitting at tables talking amongst themselves.

RONNIE ASHMORE

As he passed behind the stranger, the man turned slightly, sticking a boot into Long's path. He couldn't avoid tripping over the stranger's boot. As he fell, Long was shoved in the back causing him to fall harder than he would have.

Long landed on the sawdust floor hard, the breath knocked out of him. He laid there for a moment to gather his wind, then stood to his feet and faced the stranger. He was taller than Long's six foot by a head, and was about the same build.

"I got a message to deliver to you." the stranger said.

"Better tell me now because it will be hard to understand you when you have no teeth," Long said.

The man laughed a short laugh, then said,

"You're crazy. Nobody beats me with fists."

Long had made a mistake, he had talked too much instead of just doing. The man was smiling and he stepped closer to him. Long had no choice but to meet force with force.

11

Silas, from behind the bar, put his towel down and looked at the two men staring each other down.

"No fighting in here," he said.

"Not fightin' Silas, just sending a message."

"Just say it then and go," Silas said.

The man looked over at the bartender and said,

"You best remember who you are talking to, barkeep. Mister…"

Long hit him. Flush on the jaw while the man was talking. He felt the bone give way under his punch and heard a popping sound as the man's jaw broke.

The man fell against the bar on his right side, the wind knocked from him from the impact of the bartop. Long stepped in, not letting him get a chance to recover, and hit him again in the face.

He grabbed a handful of tangled, sweaty hair and lifted his head up above the top of the bar, then smashed the man's face into the bar. His nose broke from the impact and blood splattered on the bar and the floor, dripping into the sawdust.

The man crumbled to the floor in a heap. Long stared down at the stranger, then over at the other men in the room, who sat silently watching. Long looked at the bartender, Silas, who was staring at him as if he had never seen anything like him before.

"Mister, I don't know who you are, but you done bit a ton of trouble off for yourself. That's Ritter's..."

"When he wakes up," Long pointed to the man on the floor. "Tell him not to come looking for me or next time he will get hurt."

"You're staying here, in town?" Silas said.

"I am. I won't be hard to find."

Long walked out of the saloon. He didn't know what trouble lay ahead or how many of Ritter's men he'd have to face to find the truth. But he knew he would find it.

He was just walking, lost in thought, and looking around the town. As he approached an alleyway by the restaurant a voice called out and broke his concentration.

Young, female. That was Long's first thought. His second thought was who could it be. He looked the way of the alley and saw the young waitress.

She motioned him over toward her, she looked both ways to make sure they weren't seen. Her dark hair piled on her head in a loose bun bounced back and forth as she motioned for him to hurry.

Long stepped into the alley and followed her into the deeper shadows, hidden from the sunny street.

HOMECOMING

She looked both ways down the alley, then said,

"Did you really beat up Morgan in the saloon earlier?"

"I beat up somebody, he didn't tell me his name."

"I'm telling you his name now. Morgan Ritter."

he said nothing, just stared at her.

"You're not getting it are you?"

Her dark hair jostled with each word.

"Morgan Ritter. As in Ritter's son. As in, you're in trouble, mister."

"I'm not worried about trouble. It seems trouble has dogged me my whole life."

"Once Ritter finds out what you did to his son, he will dog you like you ain't been dogged."

She shook her head. He said nothing. Mainly because he didn't know what to say.

He played it off to this pretty girl like he wasn't worried, but in a way he was. He wanted to confront Ritter and find the truth, but he wanted to do it on his own time. Now, it seemed that the schedule was thrown off.

"What's your name?" he said.

She looked at him for a moment, shook her head again, and said,

"Frannie."

RONNIE ASHMORE

"Well, Frannie, I plan on not being hard to find if Ritter or his men want to push the issue."

He hoped he sounded more confident than he felt.

12

Long sat in his hotel room thinking of what his next move could be. He knew he had no friends in town, no one he could count on to help if he needed it.

But wasn't that the way it had always been? No matter where he drifted to after leaving this area when he was young, it seemed he was always on his own. Now it should be no different.

The waitress, Frannie, crossed his mind. He felt a smile forming on his face and quickly stopped it from completing. He had no business thinking of her at any time, especially now.

But why would she risk telling him about Morgan Ritter? It didn't make sense. Who was she? He wanted to know more.

He happened to glance out the window to the street below. He saw them. Ritter and his men. There were five of them together. Two were carrying Morgan to a wagon. He watched as they lay the wounded man in the bed of the wagon.

Ritter looked up toward the hotel window. Long knew with the curtain closed he could not be seen. He drew the curtain back fully and stood there watching Ritter watch him.

RONNIE ASHMORE

The expression on Ritter's face was anger, rage actually. He said something to one of the men, who then looked up toward the window too.

The man had on rough clothes and a dark hat. He didn't look like a typical cow hand. The gun he wore low on his right hip looked well used, even from this distance.

The other men were all of the same type, though he couldn't see much of their features. They just all had the same look to them.

For the first time, it occurred to Long that he might be in trouble. Trouble enough that he may die trying to prove something to himself.

Ritter said something and his men mounted their horses, Ritter stepped up on the wagon seat next to the one he had talked to earlier. They all looked my way again as they rode out.

Long closed the curtain and decided on his next move. He checked the loads in his pistol and went in search of food.

As he stepped out of the hotel, he stood on the porch looking around at the town. The town only had one restaurant and though Frannie and he had argued, he still had to take meals there.

He walked along the street noticing the sun was setting. It was later in the day than he had thought. He was lost in his thoughts and too late he realized what he was hearing.

HOMECOMING

The sound of hooves running along the dusty street brought him to his senses. He turned to see two horses charging toward him. The riders were sitting tall in the saddle, one of the riders had a rope, he shook out a loop and was swinging it over his head.

He caught just a glimpse of the two horsemen, the one with the rope was Ritter's man he had spoken to prior to leaving town earlier with his wounded son.

He threw the rope toward Long. Before Long could react, it dropped over his shoulders and was pulled tight around his chest. The rider dallied the rope around the saddle horn, then spurred his horse. Long was jerked off his feet to the ground, unable to resist he was dragged along the dirt street through the dung and urine.

Long lost track of the second rider. All he could focus on was not hitting his head as he was being dragged along. He could feel his arms and chest being scrapped raw, he could feel the blood from cuts and scratches. At some point as he was being dragged down the street, he lost consciousness.

He awoke spitting and choking on water that had been thrown in his face. Long knew instantly his arms had been tied above his head. He could smell manure and horses. As he gathered his wits he realized he was hanging from a beam in the livery stable, his toes barely touching the ground.

RONNIE ASHMORE

He had one boot on, one boot off. His clothes were torn and ripped to rags. He was bleeding from several cuts and scrapes on his face and body. Just breathing caused searing pain.

As he tried to focus his vision, he realized he had blood from a cut on the scalp running in his eyes making it hard to see. A hand slapped him hard on the cheek causing his head to jerk back painfully. He spun in the air by his arms as his feet lost contact with the ground.

Another hand stopped Long from spinning. He heard two men laughing and was able to focus enough to see who it was.

"We gonna kill 'im, Tom?"

The one called Tom was the man Ritter had spoken to at the wagon earlier. He filed the name away.

"Ritter don't want him killed in town. Wants to make a lesson of him to folks here."

"Even better."

Tom hit Long hard in ribs that were already hurting. The other one joined in and together they took turns beating on the tied-up man. Each enjoying their work.

Long held on as long as he could, then somewhere in the starlights of pain and agony, he mercifully lost consciousness again.

13

Long came back to the living world slowly. He had cobwebs in his mind that weren't clearing as fast as they should have. He moved his left arm and pain shot through his entire body. He tried moving his head and the blinding pain kept him still. He only managed a moan, weak sounding and feeble though it was.

He was lying on a bed; in a room he had never seen before. He tried to look around but was only able to see through one eye. The left one seemed sealed shut.

A sound came from the lone window, he attempted to look that way but couldn't move enough to see. A face appeared before him, blurry then in focus. She stared down at his face. It was the waitress, Frannie.

He relaxed onto the pillow, and tried to swallow. Even that hurt terribly.

"You survived. I was wondering if you would wake up."

He looked up at her with one eye.

"How long have I been here?"

"A week, thereabouts."

"A week? The men who did this…"

"Were Ritter men, probably in retaliation for what you did to his son."

"I remember," he nodded his head slowly.

The pain seemed to be all over his body, from head to feet. He recalled being dragged behind the horse through the street, then hung from the rafters of the livery barn and beaten.

He coughed. A moan escaped his throat before he could cut it off. Frannie was looking down at him, her forehead was crinkled as her eyes were wide, worry was plain to read on her face.

"Why are you helping me?"

"I guess I'm a fool for lost causes and stray animals," she said, sitting down in the chair by the bed.

"Which one am I?"

"Both, it seems."

Long looked at her, wanting her to explain. After a long silence she said,

"You came here to settle down because this is your home, so you say. Then you start a war with the most important family in the county and never blink an eye."

"You make me sound reckless."

"You are. Very reckless, indeed. First, no one is going to support you in this fight if they don't know who you are, Mr. Lincoln. Let's start with your name. What is it?"

HOMECOMING

Long stared at her for a moment, his head pounding from listening to her talk and her voice was irritating.

"What difference does it make if no one will know the name anyway?"

Frannie stood, staring down at Long. She could feel her temper rising. She struggled to control it. She walked to the door but as she went to open it, she looked back at Long.

"At least it would be correct for your tombstone."

"Jim Long," he said.

Frannie didn't answer, she left the room slamming the door hard enough it vibrated the window on the other side of the room.

Long was soon asleep, Frannie and her anger shortly forgotten.

14

The past few days had been hectic at the Ritter Ranch. Ritter had instructed his men to keep tabs on the progress as the man recovered from the attack in town.

Ritter had ordered his men to attack the troublemaker after he had attacked Morgan, Ritter's son, in front of everyone in town.

That sort of disrespect would not stand. It had to be answered swiftly and in the open. If nothing else, so that no one else in town would decide to defy Ritter or his men.

Ritter sat at his desk in his office turning the name over in his mind.

He had become aware of the stranger when he found out from some of his men that the stranger had taken over an abandoned cabin along the river. For almost a month Ritter had waited to catch a glimpse of the stranger.

Then one day he did. He had ridden to the once abandoned cabin to talk to the man, but never made it all the way.

He had caught sight of the stranger working in the yard of the cabin. He knew instantly that the young man was trouble. And trouble needed to be dealt with.

HOMECOMING

Burning the cabin and not making sure the man was dead was the first mistake. Leaving him alive seemed to be costing Ritter more than he intended to pay, so to speak.

Ritter opened the humidor on his desk and fished out a fresh cigar. Biting the end off, he struck a match and inhaled slowly, letting the smoke linger in his mouth.

A knock on the door interrupted his reverie. He exhaled the smoke forcefully and shouted for whoever to come in.

The door opened and his foreman Tom Rikard entered the room, closing the door behind him.

"Update?" Ritter said, sitting forward in his chair.

"He is still alive. He is in a bad way, though."

"Good. I want him to live long enough to know he messed up coming to this valley. If Morgan had died he would be long dead by now."

"We know a name?"

"Yes, sir. Jim Long."

"Jim Long. Is he still down and out of commission?"

"Yes, sit, Frannie is nursing him, taking care of him over at Doctor Nelson's."

Ritter's face seemed to melt for a moment, then anger replaced the look of shock.

"Why? Does that girl not know he attacked Morgan?"

RONNIE ASHMORE

"I don't know what she knows, sir. I can try to talk to her but you know how she can be," Tom said, not really liking the idea of talking to Frannie.

Ritter was silent for a long moment. Then he looked at his foreman and shook his head.

"No, Tom. I'll talk to her, if she'll listen."

Tom nodded, then left the room relieved he wouldn't have to face that tiger.

15

Frannie was wiping down tables from the supper rush when the bell above the door rang out. She looked up, surprised for a moment, to see Ritter standing in the walkway watching her.

"Mr. Ritter, if you are hungry, we have some beans left," she said as she folded the towel she was using.

"I got beans at my place. I came to ask you a question."

Frannie looked at him a moment, then said,

"I was wondering when you would be by to ask."

"That man hurt Morgan. Made threats against people in this valley. Don't you even care?"

Ritter had stepped closer to Frannie as he spoke. He was an imposing man, not in height as he was average height, but in the way he carried himself. She stepped back a step.

"Only threats were to you, Mr. Ritter. Morgan should never have tangled with him."

Ritter stared at her, speechless for a moment. He couldn't believe he was hearing what he was hearing.

"I want him out of this valley as soon as he can sit a horse," he said.

"He won't scare easily. Are you prepared to make good on the threats you've made?"

"Nevermind me. What have you told him about life in Leonville?"

"Nothing at all. If I could leave this place, I'd set fire to it just like you set fire to his cabin."

Ritter's head jerked up in surprise. He stared at the young woman for a moment.

"You talk mighty free for a woman. I suggest you keep your mouth shut from here on."

Ritter turned and walked out of the restaurant leaving Frannie in the dining room alone.

She waited until the door closed, then placed both hands on the table in front of her as she fought to catch her breath. She fought the tears that filled her eyes but one fell down her cheek. She wondered if Tom Rikard would be paying her a visit after this confrontation with Ritter.

She tossed the folded towel she still held in her clenched hand on the table. She needed to talk to Jim Long. First, she needed to figure out a plan for handling Ritter. She was at a loss as to what to do.

16

Jim Long came awake slowly. The room was dark as pitch, as the curtains were closed blocking out what light there was from outside. He turned slightly in bed; the pain was less than it had been but it was still present.

A match flared; it was bright in the dark room. The face that appeared in the blooming light startled Long a brief moment.

The stranger touched the match to the candle wick on the bedside table, blew out the match, then looked down at Long for a moment. A smile played across his face.

"My boys did a good job on you, for now. If you don't ride out of this country you will get more of the same. Or worse."

Long looked at the man. He had no idea where his guns were and it didn't matter. He was in no condition to be moving fast anyway.

"You're Ritter?"

The man laughed lightly but made no reply.

"Why are you trying to kill me? What did I ever do to you?"

Ritter stood and stared down at the injured man.

"I'm not trying to kill you. Yet, that is. If I wanted you dead, you'd be dead. However, I do want you to leave this valley."

"Why?"

Long struggled to sit up, but Ritter roughly shoved him back down into the bed. Pain raced through Long's body.

"That's my business. Just remember what I said here tonight."

"I won't be pushed around. You may as well kill me now," Long said, holding his side and wincing.

Ritter leaned over and blew out the candle. The room was once again dark as a cave. Long heard the door of the room open then close.

Long sat up slowly in bed, made it to his feet, then staggered to the window. He looked out into the street.

Just a vague shadow of a man crossing the street was all he saw. He couldn't even be sure if it was Ritter or not in the dark.

Long closed the curtain. He stood by the window a moment thinking. He was on his feet for the first time in days, he was shaky but standing. He could walk around the small room and try to build his strength up a little at a time. He took some careful steps, reaching out to whatever he could feel for balance.

HOMECOMING

He would have to get stronger sooner rather than later. He knew Ritter would make good on his promise to kill him. But Long also knew himself, he would not run away.

As he walked along, he stubbed his toe on the foot of the bed and for a moment that pain was worse than being dragged behind the horse. He sat down, tired, on the bed and rubbed his toe.

Things were wrong in this valley. How wrong he had no idea but he was not going to leave until he knew.

He laid back on the pillow thinking, then was soon asleep.

17

Long came awake to someone touching his arm. The room was full of light. That was the first thing he thought as his eyes came open.

Frannie jumped back in surprise at the wounded man jerking awake so fast. He stared at her as she stared back wide eyed at him.

"I didn't mean to startle you," she said.

"You didn't."

He knew she knew he was lying but to her credit she said nothing about it. Instead, she said,

"I need to talk to you about a visitor I had last night at the restaraunt."

"Ritter?"

When she looked surprised that he had guessed right, Long said,

"He was here, too."

"Here? Why?"

"Checking on my recovery."

"Jim, I know you have no reason to trust anyone in this town, but I have been honest with you from the start."

HOMECOMING

Long looked at her for a moment, then sat up. Frannie had to move her chair back as his legs swung off the bed.

"Why? That's my question. Why have you?"

Frannie stood, then walked to the window. He watched her back, saw her head move from side to side looking at the street below.

Without facing him she said,

"I've known the Ritter's for a long time. In fact, we at one time were close."

Long said nothing. Frannie turned to face him. He sat on the bed watching, waiting.

"I was engaged to Morgan for a bit."

"Morgan? The one I busted up at the saloon? Ritter's son?" Long said, standing slowly.

Frannie nodded, took a breath, then said,

"He was a little overbearing to say the least. I broke off the engagement which caused the Ritter's some embarrassment. Anyway, they don't like me much anymore."

"So, you're helping me to get back at them?"

"No. Not really. They are bullies in this town. It's high time someone put them in their place."

"You think that is me. I have made a poor showing, if you do think that."

58

`Frannie stepped closer to Long, looking at him full force. Long was a bit unnerved by the look.

"You have them worried for some reason. I don't know why but you do."

"I don't either, but I aim to find out as soon as I am healed up enough to poke around," Long said, sitting down on the bed.

Frannie nodded. As she walked to the door she turned and looked back at him.

"When you do heal up, I would appreciate being kept in your confidence. I can help you; I think."

She left the room before he could answer. He laid back on the bed and settled in, his thoughts not far from Frannie and her bold looks that she gave him from time to time.

18

A few days later Long felt good enough to dress, slow and careful though it was, and go downstairs from his room. He wanted to see what he had missed by being laid up and healing.

The doctor was not around, in fact Long had never seen the doctor, just Frannie.

His ribs were still sore and tender, but if he didn't move too fast, they seemed to not bother him much.

The gun he wore in the holster around his waist made him feel a little off balance. He decided he could live with that. He was confident he wouldn't be taken by surprise again by the Ritter men.

Standing on the boardwalk in front of the doctor's office, he looked around taking in the whole town. He was surprised to see Frannie coming toward him.

She picked up her pace when she saw him. She stopped in front of him and looked at his torn and ragged clothes.

"I'm surprised to see you up and around."

"I felt foolish layin' in there when I'm mostly healed up."

Frannie grinned at him, then looked him up and down.

"You need clothes."

"I am on my way over there now."

"Feel like walking me to the restaurant?"

They walked slowly in silence. Long appreciated all of Frannie's help, he just didn't know how to tell her. Truth was he was growing fond of the woman and it scared him. He had never given women much thought, but now it seemed he thought of Frannie often.

He turned his head to speak to her when movement from across the street caught his attention.

Frannie followed his gaze to the general store. She looked back at Long. He was watching the woman outside the store gather her skirts and climb into a buggy.

"Who is that woman?"

"Her? That's Ritter's wife. She don't come to town very often. Odd seein' her now."

The man with her, Long didn't recognize him, slapped reins to the horse and the buggy turned in the middle of the street.

The woman glanced briefly around, then stared straight ahead. The driver of the buggy watched Long as they rolled past.

"I don't think he's too happy to see you up and around," Frannie said as she started walking again.

HOMECOMING

Long followed not saying anything. He went into the restaurant and sat down. The walk, though not long, had sapped his strength.

Frannie brought him a glass of water and a cup of coffee. He accepted both quietly.

"What's wrong with you? Are you OK?"

"What is her name?"

"Ritter's wife? Have you done gone sweet for that woman?" Frannie giggled.

She stood staring down at Long. He raised his head and shook it.

"Her name?"

"Martha. Her name is Martha Ritter. Why?"

Long repeated the name twice. Then looked up at Frannie.

"I know her."

PART II

19

"So, he saw her?" Ritter said, looking at the young cowhand who worked for him.

He tried to keep his voice neutral, to not seem too anxious.

He couldn't remember the cowhand's name, but it didn't matter to Ritter. Hands came and went around this place anyway.

He was much more concerned over what the cowhand was telling him about the stranger, Jim Long.

Ritter stood and looked at the cowhand, waiting for an answer. The man cleared his throat, then said,

"No, Sir. I don't believe he did. I wasn't going to mention it, but Tom asked me if I saw the man. When I told him he said to come tell you immediately."

Ritter rose from his chair behind his desk. He glanced once at the cowhand, then walked to the window.

From the window he could see the main house. His office was an add on to the bunkhouse, built years before. Before.

He was always a man to keep his business world a secret from his personal world. But now it seemed his two

HOMECOMING

worlds were colliding and he was unsure what to do about it.

The cowhand shuffled his feet, his boots breaking the thoughts of Ritter. Ritter looked at the man, then said,

"That's fine. Tell Tom to come in here please."

The man wasted no movement leaving the office. Ritter turned back toward the window and looked toward his house. He imagined his wife, Martha in their now, cooking or preparing to cook his supper.

Ritter laughed softly. He had suggested Martha hire a maid to help with the chores but she flatly refused any notion of that. She had told him that the house he built for her would be cared for by her.

A knock at the door caused him to turn around as the door came open. His foreman, Tom, came in and closed the door behind him.

"Billy said you wanted to see me."

So, that was the young cowhand's name. Ritter briefly wondered how long he would remember that.

"Long is still a problem. What do we do about it?"

"Well, we've tried to scare him and threaten him, doesn't seem he scares easy."

Ritter sat down in his chair and looked up at his right-hand man.

"New plan. I don't want him to leave town."

Tom raised an eyebrow to show his surprise

"You don't?"

"I want him dead. He needs to die sooner rather than later. And I don't want his body found."

"Sir, you know I'd do anything you ask, so would the rest of the boys. But why?"

Ritter stood and held Tom's gaze with a look that could curdle milk.

"You don't ever get to question my business decisions, understand. If I perceive a threat to this ranch, I deal with it. Him dying is how I will deal with this threat, understood."

Tom stood silent, nodding his head after a moment, then said,

"Yes sir, I'll handle it."

20

Ritter walked to the house in the long shadows cast by the sun setting behind the hills. He felt tired and bone weary.

He thought back to when he had first decided to start his ranch here in the river valley. The Rafter T was built from his mind to what it was now through sheer grit and determination.

He had fought Comanche and outlaws alike and with equal abandon to hold onto this land and make it what it was.

What was it?

That question hit him like a punch in the gut. He shook his head as he glanced around at the two-story house, the biggest house in these parts, he was sure. The barn and bunkhouse were better and more refined than most cow operations. He had spared no expense to make the Rafter T a shining example of what could be made of this land. That's what it was.

He entered the house and took his boots off in the foyer. Martha would raise a fuss if he dragged dung and mud into her house. He had faced that wrath before but he was in no mood for it tonight.

RONNIE ASHMORE

Tonight, he just needed his wife to be near and her normal loving self. He needed to know it was all going to be fine, even with the threat from Jim Long.

He walked to the table in his sock feet. The table was set for supper. Two plates. He and Martha lived in the house alone. Morgan, who was still nursing a busted nose, lived in the bunkhouse with the hands. Ritter preferred it that way so he and Martha could be alone.

She saw him fall heavily into the chair at the table. She carried a platter of meat in one hand and in the other fresh vegetables that no doubt came from her small garden she liked to care for.

She sat both items on the table, then looked at her husband and said,

"What's wrong?"

Ritter smiled at her.

"Nothing I'm not used to," he gave her a wink.

Instead of dropping the subject, she placed both hands on her hips and shook her head.

"Ranch trouble again?"

"Isn't it always. I have to protect what is mine. What I built from nothing."

"Does it have to do with that stranger in town the boys have been giving fits?"

HOMECOMING

Ritter looked up at Martha, panic set in wondering what she knew.

"What do you know about him?"

"I know he broke Morgan's nose. I know Tom and them are worried about him. Is he the danger?"

Martha forked a steak onto his plate, then vegetables. She sat in the chair to his right and made her own plate.

She looked at Ritter waiting for an answer.

"No more dangerous than others that have caused us trouble," he said.

Martha seemed satisfied with the answer as she bowed her head for grace. Ritter recited the prayer from habit all along wanting to believe what he had just told his wife was true.

21

Long looked at Frannie. He wondered how much he could tell her about his past. He wanted to be open with her but she was also an acquaintance of the Ritter's. True, there seemed to be no love lost between them.

It still rankled that Frannie possibly had answers but he was afraid to ask the questions.

Frannie had a rare day off from the restaurant, so Long had planned a picnic down by the river. She sat beside him smiling, dressed in her Sunday dress, and looking like a million dollars. At least she did to Long.

While driving the wagon toward the river he had come up with a different idea. So, when the wagon turned off the road onto a long lane Frannie looked over at him confused.

"Where are we going?"

"My place. At least what I thought of as my place until Ritter's men burned me out."

As Long stopped the wagon in front of the charred remains of the cabin he had called home, Frannie said nothing.

He helped her from the wagon seat, she still looked around.

"How did you survive that?"

HOMECOMING

He pointed to the cedar brush.

"I hid in that all night. Then I went to town."

He grabbed the picnic basket from under the seat.

"Are we picnicking here?"

"Sure. Why not. I wanted you to see it. I was mad about this when it happened. I'm not mad anymore."

"You're not?" she said as she helped set out the food and he spread the blanket out.

They sat close to each other but not too close. Long liked her but he still needed to be careful.

"Why not?" she said as she opened the towel with the fried chicken in it.

"I have other things to be mad about. The beating, the threat from Ritter himself, the way Tittle won't enforce the law. I have a long list."

"I see," she said, handing him a plate of food.

"There is a major reason though. One that ranks higher than any of the others."

"It must be a doozy," she said, scooping some potatoes on her plate.

"Remember the other day I told you I knew that woman you said was Ritter's wife?"

She only nodded as she had her mouth full of food.

"I do know her. Know her well, too." he said.

RONNIE ASHMORE

She swallowed the food and said,

"How? From your youth? A neighbor or something?"

"Something," he said.

He put his plate to the side and looked at her. Frannie waited, chewing slowly. Long looked at her, then said,

"She is my mother."

22

Frannie coughed and nearly choked on her chicken she had just bitten into. She recovered and said,

"Your mother? Are you sure?"

"Very. My mother's name was Martha Long. I thought she was dead. How did she end up with Ritter?"

"I don't know. Are you sure? This sounds crazy."

Long picked his plate up and began eating. He felt better for having told Frannie what he had been keeping inside since seeing the woman in town a couple of days ago.

He finished his bite of food and smiled at Frannie, who had yet to take another bite, she just stared at him confused.

"I'm sure. But the only way to know without a doubt is to go see her."

"You ride out to Ritter's place; you're asking for trouble."

Long shook his head.

"The hands, most of them anyway, come to town on Saturday. They'll all be gone. I'll sneak in then and talk to her."

Frannie stood. She scraped her food into the dirt beside the blanket, then walked back to the wagon.

RONNIE ASHMORE

Long got up to follow but Frannie had climbed into the seat and was waiting. He could tell she was mad.

"What's wrong, now?" he said, walking to the wagon and looking up at her.

Frannie looked down at him and he saw her eyes were wet. He didn't know what to say next so he went and gathered the picnic items.

After he stored them under the seat and he climbed up beside her, Frannie touched his arm. He turned to look at her.

She had tears in her eyes as she said,

"I care about you Jim Long. So help me, I don't know why but I do. If you go off like this you will get killed."

Long had no idea how to respond to her statement. She cared for him? Why? He couldn't afford to get distracted at the moment. He had too much to do.

"I don't plan on getting killed," he said.

She looked at him and laughed through her tears.

"I guess nobody plans on it."

He turned the wagon around and they rode in silence back to town. Each lost in their thoughts.

Long knew what he needed to do. Wanted to do. He had to find out why his mother was still alive and the truth of what happened to his family.

As they approached town Frannie said,

HOMECOMING

"You be careful."

He could only nod in response. It was best she did not know what he was planning.

He dropped her off at the restaurant because he didn't know where she lived, then headed to the livery.

The next day was Saturday. He intended to be in the woods watching and waiting for the hands of the Rafter R to ride into town.

23

Ritter sat alone in the great room thinking and sipping whiskey. He had a bad feeling about the stranger Long. He knew the man would not back off. He would want answers. Those answers could threaten everything he had worked so hard to build.

The man had to be killed and buried and forgotten before Martha started asking questions. The longer Jim Long lived the more of a threat he was.

He took a sip of whiskey. It was a fine spirit but tonight it tasted like turpentine. He glanced at the wall clock. Just a little past ten. Morning would be early, he needed rest. He knew sleep would not come tonight.

He finished his drink, then stood, and went outside, closing the door quietly not wanting to wake Martha.

He stood on the porch staring into the night. A movement caught his eye and for a brief moment he caught his breath.

"Sorry to scare you, boss. I was just making the rounds," Tom said, coming closer to the porch.

Ritter was silent for a moment. Scared? Had he been scared? He shook the thought from his mind.

"Rounds? What are you talking about?"

HOMECOMING

"Me and the boys rotate making rounds each night. They think it's for rustlers or such. But I started this after the run in with that Long fellow in town."

This was why Ritter considered his foreman a must have around the ranch. Little things that he himself would probably not have thought of were implemented by Tom like it was second nature.

Ritter stepped off the porch and stood next to Tom, who held his rifle low in his right hand.

"Tomorrow is Saturday. I know the boys like to go town and cut loose but I'd rather they stay here close to the ranch."

Tom made a noise in his throat that Ritter took for disapproval. A brief moment later Tom said,

"They look forward to going every week."

"I know they do. And I know you do too. There will be twenty dollars extra pay in their wages."

Tom nodded, though it was too dark for Ritter to see the motion.

"That will help with their sadness. Why are we staying in?"

"I have a feeling that man will be coming to this ranch. I want us here to meet him head on."

"Sir, you definitely have a bur under your saddle for this fella. Why is he so different?"

"You asked that before, you know."

"And you didn't answer me. This time I want to know why."

"In time, Tom. In due time."

Ritter walked away before Tom could answer. He went into the house and closed the door leaving his foreman in the dark.

24

Long picked a spot on the hill overlooking the Rafter T and sat down to wait. He could see the outbuildings and the main house from where he sat among the trees and brush.

He figured the men would leave for town within the hour as the sun would set not long after that. He sipped water from his canteen and waited.

As the sun was setting Long was becoming restless. The heat of the day had turned what should have been a simple wait into a sweaty, hot chore.

He stared down into the ranch yard. There had been no movement since the men rode in an hour ago. No one was getting ready, there was no one in the yard hooting and hollering like he expected there to be for a group of men who were fixing to head to town. Nothing.

The sun set lower casting the trees in which he sat in deeper shadow. His horse was picketed a few yards behind him completely hidden as well. But to stay here too much longer was asking for trouble.

He cursed his luck. He had no idea why the plans of the Rafter R had changed but they had. There would be no one riding into town tonight.

RONNIE ASHMORE

Long was faced with a choice. Stay out in the woods, move his location from time to time and keep watch on the ranch. Or he could head back to town and regroup.

He slowly backed his way out of the clump of trees and brush. He saw no reason to head back to town. He would continue his reconnaissance of the ranch and wait his chance to get to the house and talk to the woman he considered his mother.

He thought of how that meeting might go, but only briefly. There was no need in creating a story that might not pan out.

He tightened the cinch on his horse as the sun set and darkness fell over the land. Stepping into the saddle wondered what was going on in the mind of Ritter and his men.

Why did they not go to town as was their habit on a Saturday? Would the ranch ever be left unguarded again?

Only time would tell. In the meantime he had things he could do to prepare for a meeting with Ritter and his foreman.

Long had never had a taste for killing, though he had killed when he had to. Instead, he preferred to use his brains to get out of situations, even as a deputy he only killed when forced.

He felt forced now. And the desire to kill was building within him. He wanted it, needed it somehow.

HOMECOMING

That feeling scared him more than he would ever admit. He had lived his life as an honorable man, doing what he needed to to protect the innocent as a lawman in the cowtowns or as a stagecoach guard for the railroad.

Men had died with his bullets in their bodies, but it wasn't something he was proud of.

He eased his horse down the hill on the far side of the Rafter R. He shook his head to try to rid his mind of the thoughts he was thinking.

25

Ritter walked toward his office from the house. The sun was shining brightly and the heat was enough to take a man's breath away.

Tom followed him to the office door, which was adjacent to the bunkhouse. Ritter looked at him and said,

"Can it wait?"

Tom shook his head.

"No. But we best talk inside."

Once inside the office, Ritter sat in his chair. He leaned back and looked at Tom. Tom stood in place a moment, then said,

"I went to town yesterday. Asked around. Nobody has seen Long in days."

"Meaning?"

Tom shrugged a shoulder then said,

"Meaning we kept the men in this past Saturday. Long isn't around anymore, it appears anyway. Saturday is only two days from now. The men will want to go to town."

Ritter considered what was said. He had not been off the ranch in days, wanting to stay close in case trouble showed up. But what Tom said made sense. The men could be bought with extra pay to stay in once, but if it happened too many times they would wonder what he was afraid of. He would not have that.

"Do you think Long is gone?" Ritter said, looking at his foreman.

"No one has seen him in days, like I said. Word I got from Tittle is that he just disappeared one day."

"Disappeared?"

"According to Tittle, yeah. He took that Frannie girl on a picnic. They came back to town. Next day he was gone."

Frannie. He had cursed the day Morgan had asked that woman to marry him. He cursed more when she agreed. No doubt she was a woman looking for a comfortable life so she wouldn't have to work away in that restaurant anymore.

He was glad when Morgan broke the engagement. He had heard rumors that she was the one who called it off but he didn't believe that for a moment.

"Maybe she knows where he is," Ritter said.

"I didn't ask her. She makes me nervous."

Ritter chuckled. Tom was great in a scrap or ramrodding tough men. Get him around a woman, any woman, and he became a fool.

"OK. We will all go to town and cut loose Saturday," Ritter said.

As Tom turned to walk out, Ritter said,

"I plan on talking to Tittle and Frannie while in town then I'm coming back here. I don't want to be gone longer than necessary."

"I'll let the men know that Saturday is back on."

After Tom left Ritter sat at his desk thinking. He didn't think Long would just leave. But he did plan on putting some pressure on the man to flush him out.

26

Long had spent almost a week in the woods overlooking the Rafter T. He switched locations often and was always checking for signs that men had been in the woods looking for him. So far nothing.

He was starting to get aggravated. He wanted to go down to that house and try to talk to his mother. He wanted answers.

He watched as Ritter had walked toward the bunkhouse to a small room that Long realized, a few days ago, Ritter used as an office. He saw Tom the foreman follow the boss inside, then come back out a few minutes later.

His spot on the hill and under the trees was too far for him to hear what was said or see faces clearly. That didn't stop the roars and yells of the men from the bunkhouse from reaching him.

Tom had walked in a few moments earlier, then the racket had started. Long could only hope that meant good news.

There was a slight breeze that helped break the heat of the day, but as the wind shifted Long caught the smell of an unwashed body and stale sweat. It only made him more irritable.

RONNIE ASHMORE

Deciding that nothing was going to happen today, Long retreated to his makeshift camp a few miles from the ranch. It was a nice camp, nestled between some cottonwood trees in a little wash out area by the river. Hidden from view from anyone who may have been riding cross country.

It had been the perfect spot when Long had found it days ago. Now, it was irksome to him that he was forced to spend another night in a poor man's version of a cave.

He led his horse a few hundred yards down the trail then mounted. Nudging the horse forward, he was determined to make the best of it. Saturday was two days away.

He would continue to do his diligence, moving his observation post every few hours, brushing away all traces of him having been in the area the best he could, and continuously monitoring the happenings at the ranch.

But right now he needed sleep. He led his horse into his makeshift camp, stripped the saddle from him, and staked him out near the water and some grass.

Long made his way into the washout and settled down under the makeshift cave. He planned on just sitting briefly then making his supper before it got dark. It felt good to sit for a while.

He caught himself dozing off but was unable to fight the tiredness off. He despised living in the woods and sneaking around like he was the outlaw. Ritter should be the one to feel that way, not him.

HOMECOMING

That was his last thought before sleep overtook him and wouldn't let go.

27

Ritter came from the house early the next morning. He surprised one of the hands by coming into the barn. The man was smoking a cigarette, and when he saw the boss coming, he tossed it on the ground and looked up like he had been caught doing something bad.

"You burn my barn down, son, It will be worse than you smoking," Ritter said, not stopping to talk.

Ritter walked to the stable and looked at the horses that were in the stalls.

He looked back at the young hand, who was just standing there in silence.

"Saddle me this mare here. I want to go to town. Saddle Tom's too. Then tell him he's goin' with me."

As Ritter walked past, the young man said,

"You want me to tell Tom what to do?"

"Are you deaf as well as dumb or is this a slow morning for ya?"

Ritter kept walking from the barn. He had a brief moment of feeling bad for speaking to the young man so harshly, but only a brief moment. He was still the main boss. This was his operation, his ranch. He seemed to have lost sight of that for a moment, with the trouble that he was expecting.

He wanted to hear for himself whether anyone had seen Long in town. He also wanted to take command of the situation once and for all. This was something he should have done weeks ago when Long came to town.

Tom came from the bunkhouse and stopped short when he saw his boss.

"Early ain't it?"

"I have that simpleton saddling our horses, we are going to town. Now. If you haven't had coffee yet we will get some in town."

Tom said nothing, just shrugged his shoulders as he walked beside Ritter, who turned and headed back to the barn.

"What are we doing in town?"

"Getting answers and solutions to problems."

Tom said nothing else. He knew the boss was in a mood this morning and he didn't want to face that if he could avoid it. Today was the day for being quiet and doing what was asked of you.

Half an hour later they reined up in front of the marshal's office.

RONNIE ASHMORE

The marshal was sitting at his desk leaning back in his chair, his feet up on the desk, holding his coffee cup blowing on the hot liquid.

As Ritter and Tom entered Tittle came to his feet and for a moment looked as if he had been caught loafing on the job.

"Coffee is ready gentleman, help yourselves," Tittle said.

Tom went to the little wood stove and grabbed an empty cup from the shelf above and filled it up. Ritter ignored the coffee offer.

Ritter stood in front of Tittle and stared at the man for a moment, considering his next words.

"Tittle, I have a job for you. It's urgent."

"I'll help where I can, Mr. Ritter. You know that," Tittle said, nodding his head.

"You'll help where you're told. Be at the ranch at noon today."

Ritter turned and walked out of the office without another word. Tom took one sip from his cup, put it down, then followed his boss outside.

28

Ritter stepped into the saddle and turned his horse for the restaurant. Tom followed in his wake. As they stopped in front of the cafe, which seemed to be busy with the morning rush, Tom looked over at his boss and said,

"What's the plan here?"

"Bringin' it all to an end. I don't believe Long has left the country. I think he's still around. And until I see his body I will not rest easy."

"You think Tittle will help you to rest?"

"Tittle is a useful tool, but a tool nonetheless. Even he would have a hard time messin' up what I need him to do."

They stepped from the saddle in unison. On the porch of the cafe Ritter said,

"You get coffee or grub. I need time to talk in private."

All the eyes of the people in the room seemed to look in their direction as they walked in.

Ritter glanced at Tom, who looked uncomfortable. Tom walked to a table and sat.

Ritter tried to hold the gaze of various men, but he was unable to. He ignored them instead and walked toward Frannie. She was at the counter making notes in her pad. She glanced up and Ritter could see her swallow hard.

Good. She was scared.

"Frannie, we need to talk."

"I'm busy now," she said, attempting to step away from Ritter.

He made her feel nervous and she despised him for that.

"Get unbusy," he said, blocking her path.

He nodded to the back room where they kept supplies. Frannie said nothing, just led the way. Ritter right behind her.

In the room she turned and faced the big man, hoping she was hiding her fear from him, knowing he saw through her.

"Where is Long?" he said.

"I don't know. He left after our picnic."

"What did you talk about on this picnic?"

"Nothing important," she lied. "He seemed conflicted. He wanted to leave town but was afraid to."

"You think he left town?"

She shrugged.

"I don't know. I do know no one has seen him since last week."

Ritter stared at her a moment, then said,

"I don't think he's gone. When he comes back to town, do me a favor. Tell him I will kill him."

"I will not."

Ritter laughed a slow laugh.

"Don't start thinkin' that man has changed anything around here, girl. I'm still the big bull of these parts."

"Maybe. But did you notice how the men out there openly looked you up and down when you walked in. People are hearing things and that can make a difference."

"They wouldn't be hearing things from you, would they?"

Frannie said nothing. She looked down at the floor.

Ritter walked away. He cast a glance at the men in the room. It did seem there were more hostile stares than he could ever remember.

He was surprised to find Tom waiting, sitting his saddle.

"Did you eat?" Ritter asked.

"Can't eat with people staring at me."

29

Long awakened to the sun shining brightly. He instantly knew he had slept longer than he had intended.

After he cared for his horse and made sure she was taken care of, he made his way on foot to a location he had used earlier in the week to watch the ranch house. As he settled in he saw two riders come into the ranch yard. He knew it was the foremanTom and Ritter.

Where had they gone so early? Had he missed an opportunity to go to the main house and try to make his case?

Long calculated in his mind, trying to recall what day this was.

He decided that it didn't much matter what had happened while he slept. It only mattered what was going to happen next.

He settled in for a long wait as he kept watch over the ranch. An hour later, as he was deciding to move his location, he caught sight of a rider approaching the ranch. Riding slow, as if he didn't want to be there at the moment.

As Long sat down again he saw the sun glint on something the man was wearing on his shirt, chest level.

HOMECOMING

Marshal Tittle. It had to be, Long thought. Why was the town marshal coming to the Rafter R?

He watched from his perch as Tittle and Ritter talked to each other. He saw Ritter point toward the woods around his ranch, then to some of his men.

Long chuckled softly to himself. He may have overslept but he hadn't missed the important things. They looked to be just getting started.

He wanted to move closer to the house so he could hear what was being said, but he dared not risk it. Discovery now would mean the past week was all for nothing. Better to bide his time and wait.

Satisfied, he eased from his position and slowly moved away from his hiding spot. He needed to check on his horse again. And look over his camp. He wanted to move his camp deeper into the woods, another location entirely.

As he walked his way back to the camp, glancing back every few steps to check his backtrail, he thought of Frannie back in town.

The thought slowed his pace a bit. She was a lovely woman. Full of fire, not afraid of much. A tough woman who was also gentle. She was the kind of woman he would like to settle down with and have children.

That thought struck him so hard and out of the blue he realized he had stopped walking. He was just standing in the woods, the sun shining on him, like he was a fool.

RONNIE ASHMORE

Thinking of marrying Frannie may have been proof enough of his foolishness. He shook his head and started walking again.

30

Ritter watched as Tittle rode out of the ranch house. He was becoming annoyed with the lawman. Ritter had given him that badge he wore, the town he marshaled, and the low crime in town that Tittle tried to take credit for.

Tittle seemed to have forgotten he was just a placeholder, a cog in the wheel, a minor addition to Ritter's world. And now with that world threatened by Long, Tittle wanted to argue his orders. Ritter was in no mood for arguing.

Tom walked up to him and watched as Tittle rode away to the north.

"You think he will stay on the job?" Tom said.

"No. But if he doesn't I want you to handle it."

"Maybe I better trail him to make sure."

"No, we will know one way or the other. He's supposed to report back tomorrow evening before we go to town."

"Well, everyone says the man is gone from the area anyway. Maybe so."

"I want you to go to town today and see if anyone says different. Silas will know. Make him tell what he knows."

Tom turned to walk away, Ritter's voice stopped him.

RONNIE ASHMORE

"Take Morgan. His face should be healed enough. Get a room, I'll be in tomorrow and we will talk."

Tom nodded, then looked over at the bunkhouse where Morgan was.

Ritter led the way to the bunkhouse. He entered and found Morgan sitting on his bunk.

His bandages had been removed and his face, while still bruised purple and brown, looked better.

"Ma done a good job on my face," Morgan said when Ritter stood before him.

"Let's make sure it don't happen again. I want you and Tom to go to town. Tom has the orders, you follow his lead."

Morgan stood and looked from Tom to his father.

"How come I never have the orders? Why do I have to follow Tom all the time?" he looked at Tom, "No offense meant, Tom."

Tom shook his head as to say none taken. Ritter looked at Morgan and said,

"Tom would never allow that to happen to him. You're careless, Tom ain't. Don't buck me, boy."

Ritter turned and walked out of the room, the anger apparent in the way he walked.

"What did I say that was so wrong?" Morgan said, gathering his pistol belt and other things.

HOMECOMING

"Don't worry about it. This isn't the day to question his orders or decisions. Let's just do this. We get to spend the night in town so it's not so bad."

They both felt pretty good as they walked out of the bunkhouse toward the barn.

31

As Long was walking his horse through a thicket of mesquite, trying not to get him or his horse torn to pieces by the thorns, he heard a noise from up ahead.

His horse's head came up, ear straight up, and before Long could stop her, she nickered. It was answered by a nicker from up ahead.

Long rolled from the saddle, backwards to the ground. His only weapon was the pistol he pulled from his holster as he landed.

The strange horse that caused all the commotion from in front of Long reared as the rider tried to take aim with his rifle.

The rider tried to calm the rearing horse but to no avail. The horse reared higher and neighed louder causing the rider to fall from the saddle.

As the rider fell he dropped the rifle. Long saw him hit the ground hard, trying to catch his wind.

Both horses ran a few yards down the trail and stopped to crop grass. Marshal Tittle. Long jumped to his feet and cocked the pistol.

The sound was loud in the sudden quietness that followed the horse commotion. Tittle rolled onto his knees, his hands still in the dirt. He looked up at Long. Tittle swore, hard and low.

"That won't help ya," Long said, standing over the lawman.

Tittle cocked his head back, sat back on his knees, and said,

"I guess you kill me now."

"Tittle, you got me wrong. I ain't the killer. Your boss is. What did Ritter tell you to do when you found me?"

"What do you think? He wants you dead. Don't ask me why."

"Unbuckle your gun belt, let it fall."

Tittle unbuckled the belt slowly, watching Long the whole time. When the gunbelt hit the ground Long motioned with his pistol and said,

"Stand up."

Tittle stood slowly, glancing once at the pistol still in his holster on the ground, then to the rifle a few yards away. He shook his head.

"You made the right decision. I'd kill you if I have to."

"What now?"

"Unpin the badge and drop it in the dirt."

"The badge?"

"In the dirt."

RONNIE ASHMORE

Tittle unpinned the badge and dropped it next to his gun belt. He rubbed the spot on his shirt where the star had been pinned.

"You're gonna leave the country. Ride out and never look back. If I see you again, I'll shoot you dead on sight. Understand?"

"Ride out? Where?" Tittle's voice was a shade higher than before.

"Don't care. Just not anywhere around here. Kansas, Colorado, New Mexico. Doesn't matter to me."

"Ritter will…"

"Ritter will be all done around here. Until then do you really want to ride back into the Rafter R with no gun and no badge and tell him you failed?"

Tittle shook his head.

"No, he'd kill me more than likely. Or

have Tom do it, he's the dangerous one."

"You ride out and live. Forget about this town and these people."

Slowly Tittle gathered his horse. He climbed in the saddle, looked at Long, rode away.

32

From his spot above the ranch house, he could see some activity below. Men moving around, work being done in the corral, horses being taken care of.

He saw Ritter talking to a hand next to the corral as they watched the men work. He didn't see Tom. He filed that away.

If there was ever a chance, now was the time. Long left his horse tied in the brush, hidden from view of the house.

He carefully made his way down the hill that faced the back of the house. Long knew from his many hours of watching that the back of the house was where Martha spent most of her days.

He walked fast but quietly, not wondering what would happen if he were caught. But knowing what would happen if he were caught.

He eased the back door open and stepped inside the house. Where he came face to face with Martha Ritter.

She was standing at a table, knife in her hand, cutting food. She stared at him, the knife held in the air.

Long removed his hat, and said,

"Mother?"

RONNIE ASHMORE

Martha dropped the knife, and placed her hands on her face, tears welling in her eyes. She ran to Long and grabbed him, looking him over.

"Oh, my! Is this really you after all these years? Where? What…"

Long hugged her, cutting off the questions. She hugged him back, tight.

He was overwhelmed that his mother, whom he thought long dead, was alive and well. He could feel tears burning his eyes as well.

He was also reminded he had no time to spare.

"I'll explain all when there is time. I'm in trouble right now?"

"Are you on the run?"

"In a manner of speaking. Your husband has been trying to kill me since I got to town, months ago."

Martha took a step back.

"What?"

"Morgan's face? That was me. They have been trying to kill me for weeks."

"Why? I don't believe that, Jimmy."

Jimmy. Just like when he was a little boy.

HOMECOMING

Tears of joy were in her eyes, but also clouds of doubt. Long reached into his pocket and pulled the badge out he had collected from Tittle.

"He sent his lawman to kill me this morning. I found him first. I didn't kill him but he is gone."

Martha shook her head, not wanting to believe what she was hearing.

"Not a word to Ritter about me being here. I have to go. But can you be in town this evening. I don't know how you can do it. But go to the restaurant where Frannie is working. Please. This evening."

"OK. I will figure something out. Will I see you again?"

Long hugged his mother once more then stepped to the back door.

"This evening. But remember, not a word."

He slipped out and ran up the hill toward his horse. Fearing he would be seen with each step he took. One thought flooding his mind.

His mother was alive.

33

Tom and Morgan rode into town and stabled their horses. Tom was mad and couldn't figure out why. He had been given orders he didn't like before. But coming to town like this seemed wrong. Especially when the boss wouldn't give a reason.

He would do what he and Morgan were supposed to do then go get drunk and have fun for two nights in town. At least there was that.

They were hungry and decided to go to the restaurant for some food. They entered the cafe and saw there were a few people sitting around eating.

Tom felt instantly that the mood was wrong. Usually when a Rafter R rider came into a business the men there deferred to him or at least nodded and spoke. People were staring if they even glanced up at all.

Morgan led the way to a table in the center of the room much to Tom's aggravation. A few people cast quick glances at Morgan's still discolored face.

Frannie came out from the back, saw them, and walked to the table to take their order.

Morgan had a stupid grin on his bluish-purple face that Tom found annoying. Morgan looked at Franny as she sat coffee cups in front of them and filled them from the pot she carried.

"Well, Frannie, you are looking fresh as a daisy today," Morgan said a little too loud.

"So are you Morgan, especially since your face is starting to get its color back."

The people in the cafe laughed a little too loudly causing Tom and Morgan to look around the room at the diners.

They were staring full on at the two men. No one looked away.

Tom looked at Frannie.

"Only coffee for now."

She walked back to the kitchen without another word.

Morgan leaned in to Tom and said,

"I'm hungry."

"I'm mad. Let's finish this and go talk to Silas at the bar."

Thirty minutes later they walked into the bar. Silas, instead of greeting them as he usually did, just nodded and started filling two beer glasses. He set them on the bar as Tom and Morgan stepped up to it.

The bar was empty at this early hour. Tom took a sip of beer, sat his glass down, wiped the foam from his mouth with his arm.

"Jim Long?" he said.

"I ain't seen him. Not in a week or so. Word is you killed him."

"What?" Tom asked, his mug of beer halfway to his mouth.

"Rumors say you and Mr. Ritter killed the man. The reasons vary. But I do know no one has seen him around in days."

"We didn't kill 'im,'" Tom said, sitting the glass down.

Silas shrugged, and said,

"Well, Doesn't matter. Like I said, no one has seen him in a week."

Tom looked at Morgan, who only shrugged stupidly, which annoyed Tom even more.

Tom moved off to sit at a table. He needed to think about what he had just learned.

34

Long rode into town a few hours before sunset. As he stabled his horse, he noticed two Rafter R horses in the stalls next to his. He figured they would be in town all night, which meant they would be at the bar later.

First, he wanted to talk to Frannie. He had to be careful making his way around town if Rafter R were already here.

He walked behind the buildings, keeping to the darker shadows as he went. He finally made his way to the back door of the restaurant. He knocked lightly on the door, then again.

It opened and Frannie stood there. She saw Long and instantly jumped from inside the doorway into his arms. He caught her instinctively.

He felt confused then comforted that she had missed him. And excited that she was not afraid to show it. She was quite a woman, he thought.

He released her as she stood facing him.

"The back door?" she said.

"Rafter R is in town. I don't want to be seen."

Frannie nodded.

"Tom and Morgan. They were in here earlier. Jim, listen, things have changed a little since you rode out a week ago."

"Things are going to change a lot more in a few hours."

He explained about Tittle and his face to face with his mother at the Rafter R house. Frannie listened without interruption, then when Long was finished, she said,

"Do you think she will do it? Not tell I mean, She is Ritter's wife."

"She's also my mother. That has to mean more than being a wife, right?"

Frannie shrugged.

"I've never been either."

"Someday soon."

Frannie looked at Long. Long was staring at her.

"I have a lot to do before they get to town. I better get on it. You think Tom is still in the saloon?"

"They will be there all night."

"I need to stay out of sight. They think I left the area. I need them to keep thinking that."

"Hide out at my place."

She gave him directions and told him to go in the back way.

HOMECOMING

Long hugged Frannie again, then turned and walked out of the restaurant the way he had come.

He had a lot to think about how this would go down and he needed a solid plan as he would only get one chance.

Though he had no desire to kill anyone if it could be helped, he would take no chances from here on out.

As far as he was concerned it was open season on Rafter R and its riders.

35

Frannie's house was a small frame house that sat not too far from the restaurant she worked at. Long entered the house and looked around.

It was simple but tidy and furnished with items that looked as if they needed to be replaced. The single sofa in the parlor had rips and a few tears in the seat. The chair had a smooth spot on the leather seat from too many people sitting in it over the years. All in all, Long thought it was a nice house and seemed comfortable.

He passed from the small kitchen area into the parlor. He sniffed the air and could detect the toilet water Frannie always wore. It had a nice smell. He glanced down a short hallway to his right. A door was closed at the end of the hall. Frannie's room, no doubt. He felt a sense of trespass wash over him.

He shook his head and continued to the parlor window. He glanced through the curtains at the street outside.

He could see parts of town. The Marshal's Office was to his left and down the street across from where he stood. The store where the doctor had his office above was directly across the street.

HOMECOMING

It was the restaurant he was interested in, and the saloon. He couldn't see the saloon at all and only a bit of the side of the restaurant.

If his mother kept her word, they would be eating dinner there in a few hours. In the meantime, he needed to keep hidden.

Tom and Morgan being in the saloon so early complicated things.

He had to have a way to confront Ritter at the restaurant without Tom or Morgan knowing he was in town beforehand. So, staying hidden in Frannie's house and keeping watch on the restaurant seemed to be the best solution.

He pulled a chair to place in front of the window where he could keep watch. He sat down. He felt tired, he needed rest. Living in the woods for the past week left him exhausted.

He could also smell the stale sweat and odors of his own unwashed body. He thought back to Frannie jumping in his arms. How did she not recoil in disgust at him?

The feel of her in his arms made him smile. He enjoyed her scent, her touch, the way she felt when he held her.

He shook his head to fight the sleep that tried to capture him. He finally surrendered, sleep overtaking him as his head slumped to his chest.

36

Ritter was annoyed, though he tried to hide it from Martha. She had summoned him to the house about an hour before quitting time and told him she wanted to go to town for supper. She said she didn't feel like cooking.

She did look a little peaked, Ritter admitted, it still annoyed him. He had one of the hands get the buggy ready and had made the trip to town. Martha was silent as well as they made their way toward town, she just kept looking around at the scenery as the wagon jostled along.

Ritter's few attempts at conversation had been met with either silence or short answers. He had quit trying to make conversation miles ago.

He had too many irons in the fire to worry about Martha and her moods. There was a lot going on, things being hidden from people he never dreamed he'd hide anything from. And it had been going on for a long time.

Ritter never thought of himself as old before. Sure, he could feel the years creeping up on him but he was unstoppable, determined. He was Ritter, the man who founded everything the eye could see in this valley.

He looked around the town as he stopped the buggy in front of the restaurant. He felt old. With a sigh, he dismounted. Martha climbed from the wagon, not waiting to be helped as she normally did.

What was up with her? He shook his head and rounded the wagon to open the door for her as they walked in.

There were several diners already eating dinner. Families sat at tables, men sat alone, one table had two women dining together. Ritter felt irritated knowing the wait would be longer for them to be served. He would have to pull rank and get service faster he thought as he and Martha made their way to an empty table in the back of the dining area. Martha took a seat where she could see the kitchen, forcing Ritter to sit with his back to the kitchen and to the crowd. That rankled as well.

Frannie came over and greeted them, well greeted Martha anyway. Frannie practically ignored Ritter. That irritated him too.

"Mrs. Ritter, so nice to see you. Did you come for the special?"

"Oh, yes. I cannot wait to try it, Frannie. It's been so long," Martha said, smiling at Frannie.

Ritter stared at both women for a moment, then decided to say nothing. He would figure it out later, after he ate. Frannie moved off to the kitchen.

Before coffee was even served, several men and women in the restaurant looked up and made a sound.

Ritter realized it too as Martha was staring past Ritter's shoulder toward the kitchen.

Ritter started to say something, but a man's voice cut him off.

"Mother!"

The voice made Ritter stop, look at Martha, and stare.

37

Ritter knew too late what was happening. Why the sudden trip to town. Why Martha was so silent, so distant.

Martha stood, the tears forming freely in her eyes. Ritter turned to face the voice that came from behind him.

"Jimmy?," Martha said. "When did you get back in town?"

Martha's words came in a rush, as if she were afraid she wouldn't be able to speak them.

The other diners were staring from Martha to Ritter to the man most knew he had been trying to run out of town for the past month or so.

The restaurant was silent as nobody moved or made a sound.

"About a month ago," he said, smiling and motioning to his ragged and pieced together dirty clothes. "I have had a few problems since being here. I'm sure your new husband can tell you all about that though."

Ritter made a motion to stand by placing his right hand on the table and his left on the chair back.

"Don't get up, Ritter. It's time these folks, including my mother, know what you have done."

RONNIE ASHMORE

Ritter sat back down, relaxing his hands, but staring at Long.

"What have I done, boy? You are the one that beat up my son in the saloon."

"Yes, I did. These folks, most of them anyway, know how you have been trying to kill me since I came here. Burning me out, dragging me behind a horse, beating me. All that is over."

Long glanced around the room. He saw he still had everyone's attention. He took a step forward, looking down at Ritter, then at his mother. She was weeping openly, silently.

"I thought you were dead. I didn't know you were still here," he said.

Martha reached out and touched Long's arm.

"We can talk all about this, but not here, please."

Long nodded, then looked back to the kitchen where Frannie was standing. He smiled at her. She came forward to stand beside him.

"Mrs. Ritter…"

"Please, Frannie, don't call me that for now. I need to know what is going on, what has happened."

Ritter slapped the table. It was loud in the room, the plates rattled, some people jumped. He stood and pointed at Martha.

HOMECOMING

"We will go back home and sort this out. We need not air our business in front of these people."

Martha wiped her eyes. She looked at Ritter, then took a deep breath.

"I believe I will stay here in town tonight, Joseph. I need to visit with my son."

Long could see the anger in Ritter's face. He had to hold back a smile. He looked at Frannie and nodded.

"Mrs... Martha," Frannie said, "You can stay at my place tonight if you wish."

The two women left the restaurant leaving Ritter and Long staring at each other. Ritter glanced at the diners in the room, then stomped from the restaurant.

Long watched him climb in the buggy and angrily snap the reins, heading out of town.

One more thing to do, Long thought.

38

Long walked into the bar, It was going full tilt and men were yelling and drinking and having a good time. Long saw Tom and Morgan at a table in the back of the room. Both looked to have been drinking heavily all day.

Morgan had a saloon girl in his lap, she had his hat on her head. Tom sat in his chair, silently sipping from a nearly empty whiskey bottle.

The place gradually got quiet when men noticed Long standing at the bar looking at Tom and Morgan. The change in the atmosphere finally registered with the two Rafter R men, they stared at Long a moment, unsure if what they were seeing was real. Morgan had one eye closed in an effort to focus on Long. Tom was squinting as if staring at something from a distance.

"I heard you boys were looking for me. Thought I'd save you the trouble and just come here."

Silas, the bartender, set a glass of beer at Long's elbow, he picked it up with his left hand. He was unsure how many of the men were Rafter R men or their friends. He needed to be careful.

Morgan leaned back in his chair, a distorted smile on his face.

HOMECOMING

"Well, you are still alive. I heard just today that I killed you."

Morgan laughed out loud, nervous laughter came from the other patrons.

Long sipped his beer.

"You just make sure you're sober when you come for me, Tom. That's all I ask."

He took Tittle's badge from his pocket and held it up for a moment, then dropped it on the bar.

"Speaking of killing, Marshal Tittle failed to kill me as well. Told me Ritter had ordered him to do it. His heart wasn't in it though. He rode out. Town will need a new lawman."

Long sipped his beer again. He was tired, bone tired. Too many days in the woods like a hunted animal was beginning to take its toll on him.

He set the empty glass on the bar top, then glanced around the room. He looked back at Tom.

"By the way, Tom. Your boss was in town a bit ago. Him and his wife. He left town alone though. He didn't seem too happy either. You may want to ride back and find out why."

Tom stared at Long a moment, then said,

"Why did he leave alone?"

Long shook his head.

"You will find out soon enough I guess."

Morgan stood up, placing his right hand on the table for support. He looked at Long as he swayed to maintain his balance.

"Long, you talk too damn much and never said nothin'. We got no idea why you are wanted by my old man, but orders are…"

Tom stood and placed a hand on Morgan's arm interrupting his words.

"Sure, we will ride back to the ranch tonight," Tom said, smiling. "Anything else?"

"One more thing. Tell Will I aim to kill him for burning my cabin. You gave the order Tom, I was there. I saw you. But Will lit the match."

Long turned and walked out of the saloon, keeping an eye on the two men.

As he went through the door the last thing he saw was Tom and Morgan staring stupidly at him.

39

Morgan looked at Tom after Long had left the saloon. His drunk was fast fading but he still was feeling the effects of drinking all day.

He grabbed his hat off the saloon girl's head. She stared at him silently then moved away from both men.

"What do we do now?" Morgan said.

Tom looked around the room at the faces of people that once held reverence and respect, if not fear, for Rafter R riders. He saw none of that now on the men's faces.

"Not here. We talk outside. At the livery, we need our horses."

The two men, staggering and stumbling, walked from the saloon to the livery. The sun was setting and shadows were getting long. Both men fumbled to saddle their horses, neither speaking to the other as they concentrated on the straps and buckles of their saddle.

Morgan mounted first. He took a deep breath as he adjusted his seat. He looked down at Morgan, who was still fiddling with his cinch.

"What do you think he meant that Pa was mad when he left? Why would he leave Ma here?"

RONNIE ASHMORE

Tom finished tightening his cinch, then stepped into the saddle. He shook his head to clear his mind a little. It didn't seem to help.

Tom shrugged,

"I don't know. That man is a nuisance is all I know."

"Pa would like us more if we killed him."

"We go after that man drunk as we are, we would be the ones dead. How'd Pa feel about that?"

Morgan noted the tone in Tom's voice. Usually, he would let it go but the liquor he consumed would not let it pass.

"What are you mad at?"

"We are stone cold drunk and we are heading to the ranch instead of that ol' gal's room."

Tom spurred his horse and headed out of the barn. Morgan followed behind, still not sure why Tom was mad.

A few miles down the trail but before they came to the ranch, Tom reined up and looked over at Morgan. Looked where he figured Morgan was.

The night was dark as pitch and they could not see very well. The horses were walking by habit not by choice.

"We get back to the ranch, you best let me do the talking."

"Why? Morgan asked the darkness.

HOMECOMING

"If Ritter is mad, it will be best if he takes it out on me instead of you."

"I'm the son, Tom. Don't be forgetting that."

"Yeah, I remember. I also remember how you have been a disappointment to the old man for years."

"Go to hell. Just because you're drunk talking nonsense doesn't mean I'll let a slight slide."

Tom made no reply, he put his heels to his horse and rode on.

40

Ritter slammed the door to his office, he lit the lamp that sat on the desk, turned the flame up high, and found his liquor bottle. He ignored the glass sitting beside it.

He pulled the cork from the mouth of the bottle and took a long pull. He sat down heavily in his chair behind his desk.

He glanced around the sparsely decorated room as he took another sip. This was his domain. Not just the office or the Rafter R but the entire valley. He created it like God himself had created his universe. Every detail had been planned meticulously. And it had worked so well.

Until now. Until Jim Long had ridden into the valley. Trying to run him out of the country had been a mistake. He should have killed him the first night, not waited.

It was too late now. The damage was done. How much damage Ritter didn't know yet. But that stunt of confronting him and Martha in the restaurant would not help. Not after what was said.

And Martha. Why would she turn on him so easily? How did she know that man was even in town, much less it was her son?

HOMECOMING

Ritter took a longer pull from the bottle. The alcohol was starting to have an effect. He thought back to the look on the diners faces as Long and Martha were talking to each other.

The contempt, the pity, and shame he had seen in their faces made his anger rise. He was Ritter, by God, the creator of this whole area.

He sighed a long sigh. Just as God had his plans of creation destroyed by a woman, his creation, too, had been shattered by a woman. And her no account son.

A noise outside broke his reverie. Horses? At this hour? Before he could get up and open his door, his foreman and his son came staggering in.

Ritter sat back in his chair, watching both men. They both looked as if they shouldn't be walking much less riding from town.

"What?" he said.

Tom took a deep breath,

"That Long fella, he visited us in the saloon. Told us you'd been in town, then left without Miss Martha. Then he told us Tittle rode out. Showed his badge and all."

Ritter sat silent for a moment. Tittle had betrayed him too. The night kept opening up surprises. He looked at the two men, then the open bottle in his hand. He corked the bottle and put it in the bottom drawer.

RONNIE ASHMORE

He motioned to the two chairs in front of his desk.
"Sit down. I'll fix us some coffee."

41

Long pulled his boots off and rubbed his feet. He was still sore but it was nothing he couldn't get used to.

The knock on his door made him reach instinctively for his pistol on the table beside the bed.

He opened it slowly. His mother stood in the hallway, looking to her right and left nervously. Long opened the door fully to allow her to come in.

Martha took the shawl from her head as she entered the room.

James! I'm so sorry. Frannie has told me everything about what has happened to you. What my husband has done to you. I'm sorry."

"It's not your fault."

Tears pooled in her eyes as she looked at Long.

"I thought you were dead a long time ago. Where have you been?"

"Everywhere. West mostly, mining camps, doing this or that to make a living. I wanted to come home and this area was what I always thought of as home."

Long sat on the bed and motioned for his mother to take the chair against the far wall. Martha sat down, folding her hands in her lap.

RONNIE ASHMORE

"I couldn't find our place, where we used to live. This town wasn't here then. I just settled in an old cabin down by the river. Then trouble started."

"The town was built a few weeks after Joe moved to the area. Your father was killed around that time. He was working for Joe then.

What trouble?" she asked.

"Men that work for your husband came to my cabin to kill me. I hid in the brush; they burned my cabin down though."

Martha wiped a tear from her cheek.

"It has been nothing but problems since," he said, handing her the towel from the wash table.

Martha clutched it in her hand, shaking her head slowly.

"So, you did beat up Morgan in the saloon?"

"Is he your…?"

"No," she said, shaking her head. "He is Joe's from his first wife. She died during childbirth. I raised him since he was 6 or so."

They sat in silence for a long moment, each lost in their own thoughts of the past and of the future.

Long was thinking of the present when Martha's voice interrupted his thoughts.

"Frannie likes you. Maybe even loves you, I'd say."

HOMECOMING

Long looked up at her.

"She said that to you?"

"No, of course not. But a woman can tell when another woman is in love with a certain man. And I'd say she loves you."

"I can't worry about a woman until this is over."

"How does this end, James?" she asked, standing from her chair.

Long stood and met her look.

"With death."

PART III

42

Ritter, Tom, and Morgan had sat in Ritter's office drinking coffee and talking all night. Morgan had fallen asleep on the couch against the wall.

Tom had drank enough coffee to sober up from all the whiskey he had consumed in town. Now, Ritter sat in his chair staring into his empty coffee cup.

"Boss, this is a mess we got ourselves into. How do we solve this?"

Ritter looked up at his foreman, and said,

"I still want Long dead. That hasn't changed."

"Are you serious? Everything has changed. What happened in that restaurant in front of all the witnesses. We can't lay a hand on him."

"I want to kill him myself, Tom. I want to put the bullet in his head that blows his brains out. Understand?"

"I understand. But your wife is his mother. Now, I don't know what all is going on. This obviously started before my time here, but whatever you do to him you do to Ms. Martha."

Ritter shrugged but made no reply. Instead, he stood from his chair and walked to the door.

RONNIE ASHMORE

"What's the plan then?" Tom said, standing and following Ritter to the door.

"We will plan something for tonight. Today, I need to sleep and think."

Ritter opened the door to go outside. Tom motioned to Morgan, still asleep on the couch.

"What about him?"

"Leave 'im be. The only time I don't worry about him messing something up is when he's asleep."

Both men stepped out into the bright morning light. Sunrise was not an hour old yet, but Ritter felt bone tired and sleepy.

He looked around at the ranch yard, at the men working and going on about their day. It was Saturday. The men would want to go to town.

A piece of a plan was forming in his mind already. He needed rest to fully form it, to look for the flaws.

As he walked toward the house, he considered if what he was doing was right. He snorted to himself and shook his head.

Too late to think about right or wrong. This had gone on too long to stop now. Once he took care of Long the townsfolk would remember he was the main force in this valley. And not a man to be messed with.

HOMECOMING

What about Martha? Would she forgive him for what he had to do?

It mattered little in the long run. She would take her place beside him silently or she could face the world alone. And he was confident his wife had become comfortable being Mrs. Ritter.

He entered the house and made his way to the bedroom. He didn't bother undressing, he just layed down on the bed. In no time he was fast asleep.

43

As Long pulled his boot on there was a knock at the door. He stamped his foot into the boot, then, one boot on one boot off, he walked over to open the door, his pistol in his hand.

Silas, the bartender, and another man stood looking at Long. Both men were dressed in coats and ties. Silas looked as if he hadn't worn his in a while. The other man seemed to wear his with comfort.

Silas glanced at the pistol at his side.

"You won't need that, Mr. Long. May we come in?"

Long moved back and allowed the two men to come into the room. Both remained standing. Long sat on the bed and pulled his other boot on. Silas started talking.

"This is Mark Tomey, he is the mayor of Leonville."

Long glanced at Silas then Tomey.

"One of Ritter's paid men, like Tittle?"

Tomey cleared his throat, looked down at his boots a moment, then said,

"I'll admit the title was more honorific than practical. But I understand from Silas that things may be changing."

Long said nothing. He stood and wrapped his gun belt around his waist, watching the two men.

HOMECOMING

Silas glanced at Tomey and nodded.

"Anyway, Mr. Long, we came with a few questions and a proposal."

"OK."

"If what you said in the cafe and later in the saloon about Tittle is true, then we have some reorganizing to do within our town."

Long fixed Tomey with a hard stare.

"You sayin' I made it up?"

"Not at all," Tomey said. "But if Mrs. Ritter is your mother, and if Ritter was trying to kill you, and if he had Tittle go after you, then there's a lot of questions here."

"There is no ifs in any of what you just said. It's all facts. Here's another fact, Ritter and his men are coming to town tonight. There will be trouble in the streets of Leonville. How are you going to handle that, Mr. Mayor?"

"That um, brings us to the proposal."

Long picked up his hat and moved to the door.

"What proposal?"

"You threw Tittle's badge on the bar last night. We would like you to pick it up and be our marshal."

Despite himself, Long laughed. A harsh, bitter laugh.

RONNIE ASHMORE

"Mayor, that badge is tainted by Ritter. Until that stain is removed from this town and all influence is broken, you have no right trying to find anyone to wear that badge."

He opened the door and stood to the side.

"If you'll excuse me, I am on my way out to plan for what is surely to be a deadly day in town."

44

Long walked over to the restaurant knowing Frannie would be there by now. He wanted to tell her of his visitors and get her reaction.

He entered the restaurant and glanced around the room. A few men were eating or drinking coffee waiting to start their day in the shops or wherever they worked.

It seemed all eyes glanced at him as he entered. He couldn't read their reaction.

Frannie came from the back as he sat at a corner table. She poured coffee into the cup she set in front of him.

"Your mother is in the kitchen helping fix breakfast if you are wondering."

"She is? I didn't expect…"

"She's a good woman despite Ritter, Jim."

Long nodded, then looked around the room. He leaned closer to Frannie and said,

"I had visitors this morning."

"Good they found you."

"You know?"

"I was the one that told them to go talk to you. It's a great idea. When do you start?"

Long sat back in his chair, and stared up at Frannie.

"I don't. It's a terrible idea."

"Jim Long? You talk about wanting to come home and being able to live in the area you were born in. Well, whatever trouble happens, it's going to happen in this town. To these people," she motioned around the room as her voice got louder.

"If this is where you want to call home, then by God, protect it and its citizens from the plague they have been under for years."

Before he could answer Frannie stormed off to the kitchen. The men at the other tables turned to stare at him fully.

One of the men spoke for the others.

"I run the hardware store. I used to say I owned it, but that's not true. None of us own any of our stores or houses here in town. Ritter laid out the town, sold us the lots for homes and business cheap, way cheap. In return he gets twenty-five percent of all profits from the businesses and thirty a month for the houses."

Long looked around at the other men, all seemed to be business owners. Some were nodding in agreement, some sat staring into their cups.

"All of you?" Long said.

"Everyone in this town pays Ritter to be in this town. Seemed fair years ago as no one knew any different. But now, it just seems like he's stealing."

Long nodded, though he was trying to understand he was having trouble.

"What's your name?" Long said.

"Marvin. But that's no nevermind. They say you ran Tittle off. I say good. But now we have no law here except Ritter law. The tide is starting to turn agin him for what he is."

"What can I do? They have whooped me at every turn."

Marvin stood, looked at the other men and a woman who was eating. He looked at Long and said,

"Yeah, but even a whooped dog will bite. That bite will have more effect if it is legal, with a badge, and the title that goes with it."

Marvin placed his coins on the table and walked out without another word.

45

Long finished his coffee then walked over to the now deserted marshal's office. He entered and looked around the room.

From the outside, the office looked fully formed but the empty cells and battered desk seemed hollow to Long.

Much like the town looked like a real town from afar, the marshal's office looked like a real jail but once you looked inside, it was just one man's ticket to the good life while others did the work.

Joseph Ritter was an ambitious man. He hadn't built all he had built in this valley by being meek and timid. He had seen what he wanted and he had taken it. Right or wrong.

The right had been selling town lots to the new settlers, and offering to carry the notes on all transactions.

The bad had been taking a cut of these same folks' businesses forever. There was no getting out of the debt.

True, the folks knew what they were signing, but it didn't make it right.

Long's thoughts drifted back to his father. He was a good man, an honest man. What had Ritter done to him?

A sound on the boardwalk broke Long's woolgathering. He turned to see Silas staring at him.

HOMECOMING

Silas came into the room, removed his derby hat and tossed in on the desk. He wiped a hand through his damp, thinning hair.

Silas looked around the dark room, then back at Long.

"Not much is it? We hope the next lawman will enhance it some."

"And you think I'm that guy?"

"I don't know. Hope so. It can't be any worse than what we've had," he looked at Long straight on. "Can it?"

Long smiled but said nothing.

Silas continued.

"You still think Ritter and his men will come to town?"

"They have to. His wife is here. He can't let that lay. He was insulted, his men insulted, his pride and dignity insulted. He will show, I figure."

"One more thing since we are talking about Ritter. Will, you know the man you been askin' after. He's over at the saloon right now."

"A Ritter man in town now? Why? It's early."

"He says he quit Ritter. I didn't get into it. You may want to go talk to him."

Long pushed past Silas toward the door.

"I don't want to talk. I aim to kill the bastard."

46

Ritter came from his house into the evening light. He had wanted sleep, but that had proven to be difficult to come by.

He had lain awake thinking of what awaited him in town. He had no choice in what was about to happen. His wife had betrayed him. In front of the townsfolk. Long had basically called him out and tried to embarrass him.

It would not stand. There would be revenge. A comeuppance. The thought brought a smile to his face as he crossed the yard to his office.

Morgan was waiting in the shade of the building waiting for him. Ritter's smile faded and his mood turned sour.

"What?" he said as he went to the office door.

"Tom says you have a plan to get Long back and bring Martha back here."

Ritter looked at Morgan for a long moment.

"Martha, huh? Not ma or mother even though she took care of you for all your life."

Morgan looked at the ground, not meeting Ritter's stare.

"Does that mean Long is my brother then?"

HOMECOMING

Ritter stepped closer to Morgan and slapped him. The blow knocked Morgan's hat from his head, his cheek had a red imprint of his father's hand.

"Don't ever sass me, boy. I am still the boss around here, so you go be a weak-kneed silly boy somewhere else. Understand?"

Morgan rubbed his face and fought the tears back. He would not give his father the satisfaction of seeing him cry.

Ritter stepped back, turned, and opened the door to his office. He said,

"Go get Tom and the two of you come here."

Morgan turned and Ritter shut his door. He sat at his desk feeling tired. He needed rest. Soon, he thought. Soon.

Morgan entered the office without knocking, Tom followed behind. Ritter looked at Morgan with disgust but kept the comments to himself.

"Sit down," he said, motioning to the chairs in front of the desk.

Ritter reached into his top desk drawer and pulled out a pistol. He placed it on the desk.

Tom looked at it, then looked at his boss.

Ritter pointed to the gun, then said,

"That pistol is what I used to help settle this area. That rifle on the wall," he pointed to the rifle hanging on a peg above the door, "kept the Indians and bandits at bay while

I settled this valley and made it something. Comanche ran wild through here in those days. Only a few families were here then."

There was a long silence as Ritter looked at the pistol lost in remembering. Morgan broke the silence.

"OK. That was then. What about now?"

"You're a stupid man, son. If you can be called a man, that is."

Ritter stood placing the pistol in his waistband behind his belt buckle.

"We are going to town tonight. All of us. Have the men take all their guns, all their ammunition, and all their anger with them."

He walked to the door and pulled the rifle from the pegs on the wall. He turned and looked back at the two men.

"We kill everyone who stands against us."

47

Morgan followed Tom to the barn, both men silent as they crossed from the bunkhouse to the barn.

Once inside the dark interior of the barn, Morgan looked back toward the office they had just left.

"I don't like this. Not at all."

Tom grabbed a rope from a nail in the wall.

"You don't have to like it, Morgan. You just have to follow orders. Like all of us do."

"I've had it with his orders, Tom. I don't have nothing against this Long fellow. Neither do you, yet here we are prepared to ride into town and pick a fight because he said so."

"That's right," Tom said, turning back toward Morgan, the rope in his hand. "We do what he says. There was a time that was all that mattered in this valley. Seems folks have forgot that, including you. We ride where and we fight who he tells us to."

Tom went to the stall that held his horse. He walked the animal from the stall and put the rope over the animal's neck.

RONNIE ASHMORE

He handed the other end of the rope out for Morgan to take. Morgan stared at it for a bit, then sighed, and took hold.

"You saddle mine and your horses. I got to go tell the boys to get ready. I'm sure we will be riding soon."

"I'm the son of the owner of this place, I should be treated with some respect and not made to saddle horses."

"That red mark on your face tells me you ain't quite earned that right yet."

Tom walked off leaving Morgan standing in the barn.

Morgan began saddling Tom's horse. To not do it would invite more insult from not only Tom but his father as well.

He mumbled all the while he was working. His thoughts ran wild as he worked.

He had nothing against Jim Long. True, Long had busted his nose up in the saloon. But he had been pushing Long for a fight.

And that happened before Morgan had learned the truth. That the woman he had always thought of as his ma was actually the ma of Jim Long. That still was hard to believe.

He finished saddling Tom's horse. He got his horse and began saddling him, still thinking about all that had happened.

HOMECOMING

Now, he was expected to ride into Leonville and…what exactly? Gun down Jim Long, kidnap his ma, and burn the town down.

That thought made him chuckle. It would be a good joke on his father to destroy the one thing he ever took pride in creating, his town.

The more Morgan considered his father the less he was proud of him. Morgan shook his head.

Tom was right. The Rafter R men did what they were told for one reason. They didn't have the guts to stand up to the boss.

Morgan considered that for a moment. As he tightened the cinch on the saddle, he knew in his heart he was no different.

48

Long entered the saloon and looked around as his eyes adjusted to the gloom. A man stood at the bar sipping his beer. He looked over at Long then back at his beer glass.

Only two other men were in the place. Sitting at a table in the rear of the room. They paid Long no mind. Long looked back at the man at the bar.

He was dressed in homespun and his hair was cut short under his hat. He looked no older than Long, maybe a year or so younger even.

"Been wanting to find you, Will."

"You nearly missed me. I'm riding out of here. Heading somewhere else."

Will sipped his beer. He had not looked at Long again since that first glance.

"Ritter know?"

Long stepped into the room fully facing the right side of Will. The gun side. His holster was worn high on the hip. Long noticed the leather thong was off the hammer.

Long gently removed his own leather thong from his pistol.

Will shrugged his shoulders.

"I don't know. I quit him."

HOMECOMING

Will turned to face Long full on.

"I hear you watched your cabin burn. If so, you know I didn't want to do it."

"But you did. You and Ritter's men. You say you quit. You should have quit that night."

"Following orders, that's all."

Long remembered back to the night his cabin burned. Will, sitting in the saddle and reluctantly following orders, had seemed so young and blameless. But all Long wanted at the time was to kill him.

Now looking at him in front of the bar he seemed haggard. As if he had aged years in the last few months. Long realized he had no desire to kill this man now. If he wanted to ride out then he should.

From the corner of his eye Long saw Silas enter from the back of the saloon. He was watching both men, staying out of the way.

"Where are you heading to?" Long said.

Will glanced over Long's left shoulder and grinned.

"Colorado. I always wanted to go there. Maybe Denver."

"Denver is nice. All of Colorado is nice."

"One thing I need to do before I leave though. So I know I'm leaving with a clean slate from here."

"I need to," Will's hand flashed for his gun, "kill you."

RONNIE ASHMORE

The movement and Will's words almost caught Long off guard.

Gunshots drowned out Will's last words. Long's first bullet hit Will in the chest, staggering him.

His second shot hit Will in the forehead, taking the top of his head off in a bloody mist.

Will fell against the bar, his gun falling unfired into the brains and blood next to him.

49

Martha looked over at Frannie. Both women were on the front porch of Frannie's house sitting in chairs and talking about their lives.

"Is that the start of the trouble Jimmy mentioned?" Martha asked.

Frannie listened a moment, then said,

"Only two shots. I doubt it."

"Makes me worried jus the same."

Frannie looked over at Martha, taking in what she saw. A woman in her mid-forties who had lived a relatively easy life as the wife of the richest man in the county. A woman whose dark hair, though worn in a bun, was beginning to gray.

Frannie had no idea what Martha's life had been like as the wife of Jim's father, but she knew that most people in town, the women anyway, felt sorry for her being married to Ritter. He was a hard man but all Frannie had witnessed when she and Morgan had courted was Ritter seeming to dote on her.

Frannie adjusted her seat in the chair and said,

"How do you see this playing out?"

Martha was silent so long Frannie figured

she wasn't going to answer. Finally, she said,

"Terribly. Either way I lose someone I care about deeply. I know what the womenfolk in town think, that Joseph is a terrible man and all. But that's not true. Not to me.

And Jimmy? I thought him dead a long time ago. Now to have him back seems like a prayer answered. But to have him and my husband at odds leaves me in the middle it seems, doesn't it?"

Frannie nodded.

"I guess so. But I think you may have to choose sides before this is over."

Frannie paused a moment then continued.

"I never saw much kindness from Mr. Ritter when it came to Morgan. Morgan is a good man and his own father treats him horribly."

Martha made a noise in her throat, then said,

"He's such a good man yet you borke off the engagement."

"I did. There was no way I could watch him be kicked like a stray dog day after day by his own father. A father he refuses to leave or stand up to by the way."

"Those two have been at odds since he was a young boy. Guess they always will."

HOMECOMING

Frannie said nothing else. She placed her hands on the arms of the chair to stand.

"Do you love my son? Jimmy, I mean?" Martha asked.

Frannie sat back in her chair and looked at the older woman.

"Why would you think…?"

"Please, child. A woman knows about such things. Do you?"

"I don't know. I…I am quite fond of him," Frannie said, as she felt her cheeks burning from embarrassment from the question.

50

Ritter mounted his horse, then turned it so to face the line of men behind him. Twelve men, thirteen including himself. Not much as far as an army was concerned, but it should be enough to take one man and get his wife back.

The men, all tough men in their own right but not gunmen except for Tom, sat their horses and watched the boss.

"Men, we are going into town but not to drink and be rowdy. Though that may come afterwards. We are going to eliminate a threat to this ranch and to get my wife back from this same threat."

One of the men spoke up.

"I hear'd Miss Martha is with that cafe lady, the one Morg here is still sweet on."

Laughter erupted from the men as Morgan looked around at each of them. He did not like being the topic of their jokes.

"Enough!" Ritter said. "I'll not have laughter and light-hearted jokes at a time like this. This is a direct threat to this ranch. And we will eliminate it."

"How?" another man said, "We done lost some of our toughest men to this fella. He's run 'em off and scared 'em off as it is. Including the marshal. Tom is likely the only tough nut we have in this bunch."

"Slim, are you saying the men are cowards?" Ritter asked, staring at the hand.

"No sir. I mean any one of us is solid hand on the ranch, readin' sign, and stoppin' rustlers. But none of us, myself included, are cold killers like Tom or you, Mr. Ritter."

Ritter looked at the men. He could see the fear they were trying so hard to hold in. Slim was right. None of these men were killers. Solid cowhands, maybe. Not killers.

"OK. How about this? You men ride with me through this and when it's over there will be an extra month's pay for you."

The men all looked at each other as murmurs rose from the men.

Slim looked back at Ritter and grinned.

"Well, I reckon we can shoot good enough," he said.

Ritter began to turn his horse but stopped and looked at his men again.

"Anyone who kills Long, I'll give that man a thousand dollars."

The men looked around. Whistles and shouts rose from the men. Morgan looked over at his father fighting the urge to not show his discontent.

RONNIE ASHMORE

Tom noticed the look on Morgan's face. He looked over at Ritter to see if he noticed.

Ritter reined his horse around and said,

"Let's go then."

He led the men from the ranch yard onto road to town.

51

Long came through the gate into Frannie's yard. He carried Will's gun belt slung over his shoulder, the pistol in the holster. Some local men had carried Will's body from the saloon to bury it when the time came.

Frannie watched Long come to the porch. She would never tell Martha or anyone else this, but she did feel something stir in her as he approached.

His eyes locked on hers a moment making Long want to stop or smile or something. He wasn't sure what. She had a way of looking at him that made him nervous.

He looked at his mother and smiled. He stepped up onto the porch.

"I guess Ritter will be coming tonight. Any thoughts?" he said.

"I think you should try to talk to him, Jimmy. Try to reason with him and put this behind you. He is not a bad man really."

Long chuckled.

"He's coming here with two things in mind the way I see it. To take you back to the Rafter R where he can keep an eye on you. And to kill me. I don't reckon I can reason with that."

"The shots in town?" Frannie said, watching the two of them closely.

"Will. He's dead."

Martha made a sound deep in her throat. She looked up at her son.

"Will? You killed Will. He was a nice young man."

Long looked down at the ground a moment, unsure what to say to his mother. He felt conflicted. He had long thought her dead but to discover she was still alive had been a shock. To find she was married to a man like Ritter had been disappointing.

Now to hear her speak well of a man who had literally lit the fire that burned his cabin down and who had tried to kill him made him pause a moment. Who was this woman really?

He glanced at Frannie. She was staring at him as if she were trying to read his thoughts. He looked back at his mother.

"Well, a good man wouldn't try to kill an innocent man just because his boss told him to. When this fight comes, and it is coming, you need to make a decision. Are you with me or him?"

Martha stood and looked Long, then shook her head.

"I am with you, I guess. What he's done to these people in town, I was unaware until Frannie told me. I have lived a comfortable life on the work of others and it shames me. Your father would never have done that."

"He was killed in a bar fight? Here in town, you said."

Martha nodded.

Long was silent. He was unsure how hard to push her on that topic. He decided it could wait.

"I have to get back to the hotel and prepare. There's a fight coming."

52

The clock on the wall of the hotel lobby showed it was five-thirty. Sun down was probably over an hour away.

He went upstairs to his room to get some of his things. He Picked up his rifle from the table and checked the loads, then he took his saddlebags to the bed and dumped the contents.

There was an extra pistol that he always had in the bag. That would give him three. And there were two boxes of ammunition. One for the rifle and one for the pistols.

He filled his pockets with the ammunition, one pocket for the pistol, one pocket for the rifle. Then he filled his belt loops with fresh bullets.

He took a deep breath, then looked down

at the rest of the stuff on the bed. Odds and ends. A battered book, a clean shirt. A coffee cup.

Not much to show for the life he had lived. He debated putting the things up, then grinned.

He thought, if he lived through this, he could do it later. If he didn't, it wouldn't matter.

He walked to the lone table and gathered the water pitcher to pour some into the basin. A rumbling noise made him pause.

HOMECOMING

He put the pitcher down and walked to the window. As he pulled the curtain back, he saw several horses on the street. The men were all wearing guns or holding rifles in their hands.

A glance was all he could get. A bullet shattered the glass of the window next to his head. Shattered glass flew into the room, some of the glass hitting Long in the face but causing no damage.

He instantly grabbed his rifle and ran for the door. The staircase was the only way down to the ground floor. He levered a round into the rifle and holding it at shoulder level he aimed for a point in front of him.

He made up his mind that any man coming at him would be considered an enemy. He had no idea if the townsfolk would side with Ritter or not, but he was sure none would side with him openly.

He made it to the top of the stairs. He slowly looked down the stairwell. A face appeared looking upward toward him.

Long fired his rifle, not sure who it was. His shot missed. The face disappeared and he heard a man swear loudly.

A voice from below Long's position said,

"Who the hell fired that shot from outside? Now he knows we're here."

RONNIE ASHMORE

Long yelled down to the voice,

"That's right. I know you're here and if any man comes at me I will kill him where he stands. You got that?"

Silence. No sounds at all. Long looked around at his position in the hallway. Not the best he could hope for. He needed to find a way out of the hotel.

His room faced the street but the others across from him faced the alley. He wondered if they had windows in the rooms.

He backed up and glanced at a room that would face the back alley. Only one way to find out. He kicked the door in.

53

Long looked out the window into the alley. There was a makeshift wooden ladder nailed to the exterior wall of the building.

Holding his rifle in one hand, he carefully stepped out onto the ladder and climbed, one handed, down to the ground. He looked around the alley for any trouble but saw nothing.

He made his way along the back wall of the hotel toward the far end of the street. He stayed close to the wall, glancing behind him every so often, looking for danger.

As he made his way, he glanced quickly back over his shoulder. He turned and was surprised to see a man standing there.

The stranger was just as surprised as Long was. They both stood still for a second, then gathering his wits, Long swung his rifle into action, firing from the hip, his left hand steadying the gun.

Long's bullet hit the man low in the right side. He fell to the ground, moaning in agony. His pistol was still in his holster.

Long worked the lever on the rifle and loaded a fresh round into the chamber. He kept the rifle on the stranger as he stepped up closer to him. He looked down at him for a moment, then reached down and unbuckled the man's gun belt.

He slung the belt over his shoulder, then removed the pistol. He placed the gun in his waistband next to his spare. Then he removed the extra cartridges from the loops of the belt.

He tossed the empty gunbelt on the man's stomach causing him to moan louder in pain.

"My God, man. I need a doctor. I'm gonna die here."

"You'd have left me to die here if you'd been a little faster. You almost had me. Too bad for you."

Long stepped over the man's outstretched legs to walk away, the man grabbed at Long's boot.

"You really leaving me here?"

Long kicked the man's hand away.

"Hope you die slowly."

Long walked away. He didn't look back. He did cuss himself for being so easy to sneak up on. He reminded himself to be more careful and watchful.

He walked along the back alley a little faster. He knew the shot was heard and it would bring more Rafter R men to the alley.

Long reminded himself that in spite of what Silas or the mayor or anyone else said behind Ritter's back, that this was still a hostile town. Any man he saw on the street had to be considered an enemy. Either a Rafter R man or a Ritter supporter.

He had shot and probably killed one man. How many more would die before this was over?

Long walked on.

54

After the shot at the hotel window that broke the element of surprise, Ritter sent a man into the hotel. The man quickly returned saying Long knew he was there and had seen him.

After a moment of thinking Ritter sent a man around the hotel into the back alley. Long may have the edge now but hopefully his man could catch him coming out the window or something.

As the man went around the corner, Tom looked at Ritter and said,

"You think one man is enough?"

"We will know in a moment."

A gunshot sounded. When the hand didn't return Ritter said,

"Guess not."

Tom shook his head as he dismounted. The other men followed Tom's lead.

"All right, Long knows we are here. He probably killed Jake just now. Keep an eye out for him. If he sees you first, you're probably a dead man."

HOMECOMING

Morgan was the last to dismount. He looked from Tom to his father. He pulled his rifle from the saddle scabbard and said,

"What's the plan, Pa?"

Ritter glanced down at his son.

"Well, look who's decided to take a hand. I am going after my wife while y'all look for Long."

"I'll go with you," Morgan said as he stepped into the saddle again.

"Morgan," Tom said.

"Pa's right, Tom. She is as much my mother as she is his."

Ritter turned his horse and eased beside Morgan.

"I'm glad to hear you say that. Let's go get her. That waitress is hiding her I expect."

The two men rode off toward Frannie's house each lost in their own thoughts.

Morgan, his rifle across his lap, was watching all sides of the street for Long. He was also thinking about how life in this country was going to change after today.

Sure, the Rafter R had killed men who came after the family before. Comanche, rustlers, bandits. But nothing as blatant as the son of the matriarch. That's what Martha Ritter was, the matriarch of the Rafter R. She had married his Pa before Morgan was a year old. He couldn't remember his real ma. He could remember Martha.

Ritter looked over at Morgan. That was his son. Not always the smartest or the toughest but he was here now standing shoulder to shoulder with him and the threat he faced.

Ritter looked ahead, a smile on his face. He was thinking of taking Martha home.

55

Martha saw the two riders coming up the street. She had heard the gunfire earlier and now seeing the two men she knew her son lay dead in the street. Tears welled in her eyes as she stared at them.

Frannie stepped up beside her. Seeing tears in Martha's eyes caused Frannie to tear up as well.

"Your husband looks as if he's leading a parade."

Martha couldn't disagree. Joseph sat his horse straight as a pole, riding with a slight smile on his face.

Only Morgan looked wary like he could be attacked any moment. He held his rifle across his lap and his head was constantly moving.

That gave Martha a glimmer of hope. Just a glimmer though.

Martha stepped out onto the porch and watched the men ride up. Joseph reined up at the gate, looked around, then said,

"Martha, it's time to come home."

"Joe, aren't you angry with me?"

Ritter chuckled.

"No, I am not angry. Let's just go home and we can picnic in our favorite spot and talk about all this."

"We have no picnic spot."

"Sure, we do. Down by the river. Under the pecans and cottonwoods."

Martha screamed. Morgan's horse was startled by the sudden noise. He fought to control the animal.

He looked at his pa. Martha was backing up and heading into the house again. Ritter went to dismount but Morgan was on the ground first.

"Pa, I'll go see what's wrong."

He tossed Ritter the reins and moved onto the porch in a couple of fast steps. He went into the house to find Frannie and Martha arm in arm.

Martha was crying. Frannie was trying to calm her. Frannie looked at Morgan.

"What did your father say?"

"Nothing. Wanted to take her home and go on a picnic."

"A picnic?" She turned back toward Martha and held her at arm's length. "Why are you crying over a picnic?"

"That's how he killed her, I am sure of it now," Martha said, still crying.

"Killed who?" Frannie said.

"Down by the river in the trees. He always said she drowned; he told me it was her picnic spot. And he hated picnicking. One day she went swimming and she drowned.

HOMECOMING

But I don't believe that anymore. Because he also said she slipped off a rock she was standing on."

"Martha? Who are you talking about? You sound like a crazy woman."

"It makes no sense to me either. But why would there be two stories for one incident? I remembered just now."

Morgan, who had been standing in the room watching, took a step forward. He looked at Martha, then at Frannie. He said,

"My mother! You're talking about my mother."

Martha looked at Morgan. She broke free from Frannie and grabbed Morgan in an embrace.

"I am sorry. I didn't know until now. It hit me out there. My husband, then your mother, within a week of each other. No coincidence. It was his plan."

Morgan held Martha a moment longer then let go.

"My father killed my mother and Jim Long's father so he could marry you?"

A noise from outside made them turn to look. Ritter stood on the porch watching them.

56

Long was wary now. As he moved along between the buildings and tried to limit his risk of exposure, he felt like he was moving too slow, a snail's pace.

He had no idea who the man he had shot and left back there was. Although, he was sure he was dead by now.

There were others. Ritter's men. Including Ritter himself and his foreman, Tom, who was probably the deadliest of them all, according to rumor.

Long crept up to the mouth of the alley and looked, one eyed, into the street. It took a moment for what he saw to register.

A group of men sat their horses and were talking amongst themselves. They seemed to be in no hurry.

Long recognized Tom. He had seen a few others from afar when he was watching the ranch from the hills but didn't know their names.

Why would they not be hunting for him? Where was Ritter and Morgan?

His mother! The thought hit him like a bolt of lightning. He had to get to Frannie's house and check on his mother.

HOMECOMING

The path to get to Frannie's was back the way he had just come. He silently moved back into the alley hoping not to be discovered now.

He retraced his steps back to the rear of the hotel to the now dead man he had shot. Long didn't pause or look at the man as he stepped around him continuing on his way to Frannie's house.

He came to a small church that was a few blocks from Frannie's house. He cut across the church yard being sure to keep the building between himself and the main street where the riders were.

As he walked, rifle in hand, eyes scanning, a single gunshot echoed out from in front of him. It startled him for a moment, then he walked faster toward the sound.

As he rounded the corner of a house a few hundred feet from Frannie's own house, he saw Ritter dragging his mother out onto the porch of Frannie's house. He was yelling something Long couldn't understand.

Long raised his rifle and took aim. He couldn't risk the shot. The distance was too great and the jerky movements of both Ritter and his mother made such an attempt too risky.

Long lowered his rifle and began running. Ritter saw him and squeezed a quick shot from his pistol. The shot went wild. Long kept running.

RONNIE ASHMORE

Ritter grabbed Martha by the shoulders and hit her hard across the jaw with a closed fist. Martha crumpled into Ritter's arms.

Ritter tossed her roughly across the front of his saddle then stepped up into the leather. He reined his horse around and spurred the animal onward.

In the opposite direction of where his men were sitting and waiting for him back in the town.

One thought flooded Long's mind as he continued to run toward the fast-running horse. Where was Frannie?

57

Long stepped up onto the porch as Frannie and Morgan came staggering out of the house. Frannie was helping Morgan as he leaned on her for balance.

Morgan locked eyes on Long, a man he had until recently considered a mortal enemy who should be shot on sight. Morgan shook his head and pointed behind him into the house.

"My pa shot me. I tried to get the drop on him but he was quicker than me."

Long looked at Frannie skeptically, then back at Morgan.

"Why would your own pa shoot you?"

"Long story. The bottom line is ma is in trouble and you have to help her. I'll get the bleeding stopped and be on my way to the ranch. But right now, you have to go."

"There's men back there in town wanting me dead. What do…"

"I suppose they are sitting their horses in the middle of the street trying to figure out what's going on. Tom knows. So do I."

Long considered what Morgan said for a moment, then said,

RONNIE ASHMORE

"Is that your horse?"

"Take him and welcome to it. You have to get to the Rafter R and get our mother away from him before he kills her too."

Long had a dozen questions he wanted to ask. But there seemed to be no time to find the answers. Morgan was bleeding from a leg wound he needed to care for. And his mother was being dragged to her death by a man she loved above all men.

"OK. Can you control the Rafter R men in town?"

"Tom can. Please go now."

Long turned to go to Morgan's horse. Frannie's words made him pause a moment.

"Jim, be careful, please. I want you to come back safe. So, we can picnic again if we want to."

He turned to look at her. There were tears welling in the corner of her eyes. He looked away. He could not be distracted by Frannie now.

He shoved his rifle in the empty scabbard and stepped into the saddle.

He turned the horse and put spurs to it and headed out on a fast run.

Another horse came from the other end of town, alone, seeming to take its time in walking toward them.

HOMECOMING

Tom reined up and looked at Morgan's bleeding leg. He nodded toward the fast-disappearing rider ahead of him.

"Long shoot you, Morg?"

Morgan let go of Frannie and stood on his wounded leg, wincing from the pain. He hobbled two steps toward Tom.

"Pa shot me Tom. Not Long. Pa. And he took Martha by force back to the ranch."

"Long is going after them, huh?" Tom said looking off where Long had ridden.

Tom didn't wait for a reply. He spurred his horse forward and followed the trail back to the Rafter R.

Part IV

58

Martha came slowly to consciousness. Her first thought was the rough jostling she was experiencing. Then she became aware of being across the back of a horse on her own front side.

It all came back to her. Her husband had hit her hard in the face. It must have knocked her out. She felt a hand on her back helping her to balance as the horse ran along. It was the most uncomfortable she could remember ever being.

Joseph had shot his own son. That memory jarred her a moment. Was Morgan dead? What about Frannie? What was going to happen to her?

Her mind was in a panic as her thoughts raced. She fought to control herself. She knew she had to be calm and keep her senses if she were to survive. And in the end even that might not help her live through this.

The horse slowed. She felt the rider lean back in the saddle as the horse came to a stop. Holding her in place across the front of the saddle, he dismounted then lifted her from horse to the ground.

They were in the ranch yard. The bunkhouse and barn were in front of Martha, the house behind her.

RONNIE ASHMORE

"I figured you were awake," he said as he held her by the shoulders and looked at her.

He touched her cheek with his left hand. Martha winced from the pain, her head was throbbing, she felt sick.

"Never have you ever defied me before, Martha. I told you to come on home and you ran into that hussy's house. You should have listened."

"Frannie is no hussy."

Her voice sounded weak even to herself. But she could figure nothing else to say at the moment.

Ritter looked at her, then laughed. When he gathered himself, he said,

"Well, any rate. I don't want you defying me again. I sure don't want you keeping company with Frannie Johnson. She is no friend of this ranch."

She broke free from his hold.

"You heard what I told her and Morgan. You shot your own son. For God's sake what is wrong with you?"

"I heard. You're plumb loco. That's what I think. And Morgan was going to shoot me because of you. I had to shoot him."

Martha could sense no remorse or sadness in his voice. He was just reciting facts, like how many cattle he had on the ranch.

"Is he dead?" she asked.

HOMECOMING

He shrugged a single shoulder as a response. As though the answer didn't matter to him too much.

"I'm not crazy, Joseph. I just smartened up to what I have been ignoring for years. You are not who I thought you were."

He chuckled and shook his head.

"I've always been what I am."

59

Long was having no trouble following the trail. RItter was heading for the ranch. He was aware of a rider on his back trail, following along at a gentle pace, not trying to catch up but not letting Long get too far ahead.

The rider was too far back to make out who it was. He doubted it was Morgan with his leg wounded as it was.

That only left Tom. The most dangerous of all the Ritter men. Whatever happened at the ranch, Long reminded himself he would have to consider Tom.

There had been a shift in the events and happening of the day. And Long still wasn't sure where he fit in the new scheme of the way things were going.

The tide had seemed to turn on Ritter and the Rafter R. The townsfolk had heard more rumors and gossip in the last few days, some of which corroborated their own suspicions.

Long took to the brush to survey the ranch house. It was one of the posts he had used the week he had kept watch before.

He dismounted and walked slowly through the trees. He knelt down beside a pecan tree and looked the ranch over.

HOMECOMING

His mother was standing, Ritter was standing next to her. They looked to be talking things over.

Long needed to plan a way to get down there without being seen. He was forced to wait until he knew where Ritter was going to hold up at. Then he could make his plan.

Ritter had to know he would be pursued. Either now or later by the county law. His best option was to handle whatever he needed to now so he could control the way the story was told later.

If Long were to die no one in town would go against him. Would Martha survive? Would Ritter kill his wife?

If the choice was the ranch or his wife, Long figured he knew what Ritter would choose.

A horse and rider broke Long's thoughts. Tom came riding easy into the yard and reined up in front of his boss and wife.

Ritter looked at Tom a moment, said something in which Tom replied. Tom dismounted as Ritter looked around the hills and brush surrounding the ranch.

Long felt he looked right at him. Why not? Tom probably knew where he was hiding. Long cussed himself for being careless again. Much more of that it wouldn't matter what story was told because Long would be dead.

Long considered his choices. A plan was starting to form. Tom may know where he was but he didn't know where he would be.

Tom remounted his horse and turned it away toward the hill where Long now stood. Ritter took Martha's arm and led her to his office by the bunkhouse.

Time to go, Long thought. He went to his horse.

60

Long rode in a wide circle around the direction Tom was now heading. He wanted to be in front of the foreman and get to the ranch yard first.

He had no desire to face Tom with a gun. He was not sure he could win after listening to all the talk about the man. But if he had to…

He took the rough country at a slower pace than he wanted because he didn't want to get his horse hurt. But the animal was familiar with the smells and sights of the area, so he wanted to go faster toward the barn.

Long held him back and controlled the pace.

He came to a hill and reined up. He was on the backside of the house. The bunkhouse on the other side was hidden from view.

He looked around for any sign of Tom. There was nothing. Long dismounted and tied the reins around a tree. The horse stood still, only his tail was swishing.

Long walked down the hill with his rifle in his left hand. His eyes were scanning everywhere looking for danger.

As he approached the steps that led to the back door of the house, he stopped. What was that he'd heard? Maybe the wind or the house settling. He didn't know.

RONNIE ASHMORE

He took another step. Around the corner walked Tom, who stopped and looked at Long smiling.

Long stopped in his tracks and for the third time that day cussed himself.

"You got here early," Long said.

"Figured you had to come to the house sooner or later. Not that hard to outsmart you, boy."

Long sighed, then shook his head.

"Seems you and your men have been doing that since you torched my cabin."

"About that. It was all business. Boss said to do it. I do it."

"What about now? You know he shot his son in town, took his wife by force, and are in his office."

"Morgan is useless. He should have been shot before now. And the arguing of a man and his wife ain't none of my affair."

Long hoped to keep him talking in order to figure a way out of the jam he was in. He held his rifle in his left hand pointed downward. He may as well have left it in the saddle scabbard for all the good it would do now.

His pistols. He had two loose in his waistband, one in front and one at his back, and his belt gun. He wondered if he could get to them. Tom stood ready, his hand resting on the butt of the gun in his belt.

HOMECOMING

"You really gonna kill the son of your boss's wife?"

Tom chuckled.

"Boss says it's worth a thousand dollars. He says it, I do it."

Tom's hand tightened on the gun butt. Long reacted to the sudden tensing of Tom's hand. Long drew his belt gun and fired two shots that sounded as one.

The bullets hit Tom high in the chest causing him to jerk back. He fell to the ground; he kicked his left leg once then died.

Long stood there a moment. Unsure if he had actually beat the man. He holstered his pistol. He shifted his rifle to both hands at the ready.

His job wasn't finished yet.

61

Ritter sat in his chair at his desk staring out the window toward the house and the yard in between, a pistol on the desktop silently warned Martha not to move from her position on the couch. She sat staring at her husband.

"Joe. Even if you come through this you should just go ahead and shoot me. I will not go back to the way it was before."

"Before? It's still as it always was, woman."

Martha laughed and looked down at her lap. She looked up and said,

"You hid the fact that my son was in town. You have tried to kill him for weeks. And you shot your own son. Everything is different."

He looked over at her.

"Shut up. I'm needin' to think."

Martha said nothing. She sat staring at her hands that were folded on her lap. Thoughts ran through her mind of the years she had loved this man, of never seeing the cruel side of him, and now not knowing what had happened to that man.

HOMECOMING

Ritter looked over at her. He saw a tear fall silently down her cheek. A pang of hurt passed over him. He was the reason she was crying now.

"Martha, I never meant for any of this to happen. I did everything I could to protect this ranch and you."

Martha looked at him, wiped the tears as they fell down her cheeks.

"Tell me about John. What really happened?"

Ritter was silent for a long time. He sat just staring out the window into the yard. He could see Tom walking around the main house and staring off into the hills beyond.

Martha thought he wasn't going to answer, his voice was soft as he spoke finally.

"I remember the first time I saw you. In what is now the town. It was just roped off land broken into lots then. You and John came riding up in that wagon. You were the prettiest thing I had ever laid eyes on. Still are," he looked at her and smiled.

Martha fought a shiver as Ritter poured a glass of whiskey for himself from a bottle on the desk and continued.

"I knew I needed you as my wife. John was never going to be much. I'd heard the talk that you ran your boy off to avoid the war. Morgan wasn't much younger than him. And my wife was no strong woman, not made of hearty stock like you. I knew that. So, I made a plan and followed it through."

Martha waited for him to say more. When he didn't she said,

"And?"

He took a long sip of whiskey and said,

"And nothing. The plan worked better than I could have imagined. I have been a good man to you, Martha Ritter. You know I have."

Martha started to respond to that statement but gunshots interrupted her reply. Two gunshots, close together.

62

Long made his way to the far side of the house. He looked toward the bunkhouse and the office at the end. There were no windows on the front of the office so he couldn't see anything. He wasn't even sure they were still in there.

Ritter couldn't see him unless he went to the side of the building between the other side of the house and the office. There was a window there, Long remembered.

His plan was to not be seen. He didn't know how to get Ritter out of the room though.

The only thing that made sense to his way of looking at things was a direct challenge. Call Ritter out and hope he wouldn't hide behind his wife for protection. Seemed risky.

Movement in the corner of his eye caught his attention. From over the hill came several riders and a wagon. The group was traveling fast but not hard. The wagon was in the lead and everyone else held back.

Long tried to count the riders. He lost count at eleven one time and fourteen the next. He looked back at the office. He had to do what he needed to do now. Before Ritter's men rode up and shot him down.

He cleared his throat and yelled across the yard.

RONNIE ASHMORE

"Ritter! Your man is dead. Now, let my mother go and come out and face me."

Long counted a long thirty. He thought Ritter hadn't heard him and was thinking of yelling again when the door of the office cracked open.

"You killed Tom?"

"I aim to kill you next Ritter. Come out and face me."

Long glanced at the group of riders. They were more than halfway to the ranch yard. The noise of horses and the wagon could now be heard. Long looked away, chastising himself for being distracted.

Ritter must have heard the commotion and looked out his window for a moment because he said,

"That will be my men. You got by Tom but the sheer numbers of the boys will ensure you die. I'll be out when they get here."

Long was at a standstill on what to do next. He couldn't attack and he couldn't retreat. And standing waiting for the group of men to ride into the yard was a dangerous idea as well. He needed to make a move. At least do something.

The wagon and riders came into the yard in a cloud of dust and noise. Horses were panting and riders were looking around for any sign of what was happening.

Long saw Morgan in the wagon seat, reins in his hands. Next to him sat Frannie. Long didn't know if she was here voluntarily or as a prisoner of the Rafter R men for her part in helping him.

One way to find out, Long thought. He raised the rifle to his shoulder and stepped out from around the corner of the house.

Frannie saw him as he came around the house.

"Jim," She said.

As the noise from the horses and the men faded away, Long's voice rose loud and clear.

"Anybody moves I'll start shooting. You doubt me, try me."

63

Long stood there staring down his rifle barrel at the group of men. Frannie climbed down from the wagon in a hurry. As her feet hit the ground, she turned toward Long and held out both arms with her palms facing Long.

"No, Jim. It isn't what you think. Listen."

"I'm listening. But you come stand by me over here. That would make me feel better."

Frannie dropped her arms and looked back over her shoulder at Morgan, who dropped the reins he had been holding and struggled to his feet from the seat.

"We ain't here for you, Jim. We came to save my mother, our mother," Morgan said, as he stepped carefully down from the wagon.

"Our mother?" Long said, watching everything closely, wondering what was going on.

"She's the only mother I really remember. My real mother died when I was barely more than a child. My father killed her. I know that now. Just like he killed your father."

Morgan stepped closer to Long and continued speaking.

"See, We are connected, Jim. In a way we never should have been but we are."

HOMECOMING

The door to Ritter's office flung open and Martha came out first, Ritter behind her, a pistol in his hand held in a general direction of Martha's head.

"You came with my men to stand against me. You ungrateful bastard!" Ritter said, looking at his men and his son.

Long had no shot at Ritter. His mother was in the field of fire. He looked at the other men. None had their weapons out though all had guns strapped around their waists.

I'm not a bastard," Morgan said, stepping a little closer to the steps of the office. "I know exactly who my father is. And what he is."

Martha stood still, tears running down her cheeks. Long looked at her and said,

"Are you OK?"

Martha nodded in response. Ritter jerked his pistol to cover Long.

"Of course, she's OK. What do you think?" he said.

Morgan drew Ritter's attention back to him by saying,

"How many people have you killed? I assume a lot, including my mother. It's no big stretch to think you might kill his mother as well."

Long said, "I doubt you killed all that many men. You're weak and a coward, hiding behind a woman that way. I guess Tom killed most of the men you targeted for death."

"Where is Tom?" Morgan asked.

Ritter was becoming distracted from the two men talking to him as one voice. He was looking left at Long then right toward Morgan.

"He's dead. Your brother killed him," Ritter said in response to Morgan's question.

The townsfolk, including the mayor and Silas, were still sitting in their saddles watching the scene play out. At the mention of Tom's death, Long felt dozens of eyes look his way and heard a murmur grow through the crowd. Even Morgan cast a glance at Long.

Martha used the moment of distraction to her advantage. She, still standing with her husband behind her and his gun aimed at her head, shoved back into Ritter knocking him off balance. As he stumbled for balance, she made her move.

64

Martha came off the steps in a run, stumbling and staggering for her own balance, she made it to the ground. She lifted her skirt in both hands as she picked up speed as she ran, screaming at full volume, toward Long.

From Long's view she was still in the line of fire. He had no clear shot. He could see the pistol in Ritter's right hand start to rise. Toward Martha.

Long took a step to his right as he raised his rifle to his shoulder. He wouldn't be in time. That was what he was thinking as he made his move.

A shot rang out, then Long was squeezing his rifle's trigger and working the lever as fast as he could. Another shot. Long didn't know who was shooting.

Ritter fell back against the outer wall of his office. The gun fell from his hand and clanked on the wooden steps, falling to the ground below.

Ritter didn't move. Long could see his shirt covered in his own blood. A lot of blood. Too much blood for the one time Long knew he had scored a hit. He saw his other shots pock the wall of the building.

Martha was in his arms, hugging and crying. Frannie next to him. It had all happened so fast.

RONNIE ASHMORE

Then he looked to his left.

Morgan stood there staring at his now dead father. The pistol in his hand still aimed at the onetime threat.

It was Morgan shooting; the other gunshots Long had heard. It was Morgan shooting his own father.

Silas and some of the other men moved toward Ritter's body breaking Morgan's stare. He looked over at Long.

"I only hit him once," Long said, holding his mother with one arm, the other hand holding the rifle.

"I know. You were in a bad position. He was going to kill Ma."

Morgan holstered his gun and came to stand beside the only mother he remembered. The one woman who had loved him no matter how his father had treated him.

Martha let go of Long and hugged Morgan. Frannie took the empty space in Long's arm that Martha had left.

Silas came off the steps to both men.

"He's dead. Shot to pieces, I'd say," he looked at Martha, then said, "Sorry ma'am."

Martha gave no sign of hearing Silas' remarks.

She had her head buried in Morgan's chest repeating the same words.

"I'm sorry. I'm sorry."

HOMECOMING

Morgan was doing his best to calm her down. Frannie held Long tightly around the waist and refused to let go. He looked down at her once and saw she was smiling and crying at the same time.

"We can take him to town and bury him in the city cemetery if you'd like, Morgan," Silas said.

Martha pushed away from Morgan and dried her eyes on her sleeve then shook her head.

"No. He will be buried here along with Tom. They killed innocent men and women to protect his ranch. It's only right he be buried here to see what this place becomes now."

65

It took about an hour to bury the two men. Neither one was wrapped in a blanket or put in a box. Neither one had any words said over them. They just dug one hole and dropped both men in there together. No one made an effort to make a marker of any kind.

The Rafter R men realized thirty seconds after Ritter died that the ranch had a new boss. They just weren't sure if it was Mrs. Ritter or Morgan. But either way the men, when asked by either of the two to do something, did the task fully and quickly.

As the burial party left the grove of trees where they had buried the Ritter and Tom, Morgan and Martha walked together ahead of the others.

Frannie was walking beside Long holding his arm looked at him and said,

"Shouldn't you be up there with them?"

"No, they suffered more and for longer from him than I did. There will be time for me."

Mayor Tomey looked over at Long and said,

"If that means you are staying around, we still have an offer to discuss."

HOMECOMING

"Mayor, you need to fix your town first. The payments that were being made to Ritter stop now. Businesses and residents. I don't know how you make it right but do it. You need to run that town like a real town," Long said.

"Of course, Jim. Of course. But what about law?"

"You get your part done, we let a few days go by here then we can talk about that offer. I found what I wanted; I'm not going anywhere."

After a little bit of small talk the townsfolk headed back to town with Frannie riding in the wagon. The Rafter R men headed to the bunkhouse and the barn to no doubt talk about the day's events.

Morgan, Long, and their mother sat in the great room and talked of the future. None mentioned Joseph Ritter or the past events of the Rafter R.

Martha looked at Long and said,

"Are you taking the law job in town, son?"

"I figured I would if the mayor can straighten everything out."

"So, you're planning on staying?" Morgan asked.

"I am. I came here because this is my home. Maybe not the Rafter R but this area. I plan on staying."

"Frannie will be thrilled," Martha said.

"This ranch is a big job. Too big for one man. But now brothers could run it just fine," Morgan said.

RONNIE ASHMORE

"Brothers? One man? Have you lost your mind, Morgan. I will run this ranch," Martha said, staring at Morgan until he nodded in agreement.

"You boys can certainly help, Morgan you can be the foreman, but the Rafter R will run to my specifications now."

Long smiled, Morgan chuckled.

"Well, Morg since you may have some free time, I may need help in town. A deputy, on an as needed basis."

"Work for you? You broke my nose. Are you ever going to apologize for that?"

Long considered it for a moment, then said,

"No. It looks much better now."

Martha began chuckling, then it became full laughter. Morgan tried to hold it in but he, too, began laughing.

Just before Long joined in the laughter, he thought to himself, it is good to be home.

MORE FROM RONNIE ASHMORE

Colby PD Series
Family Secrets
Colby Nights

John Riley Bounty Hunter Series
The Losing Trail
The Killing Trail
The Vengeance Trail
The Deceiving Trail
A Bullet for Malo
The Claren Range Dispute

Sam Bolton Ex Ranger
Duty Bound
Fighting Men
Crooked Trail

Other Books
Last Stand for a Bad Man
Texas: 1857

Non-Fiction
Lessons on Leadership:
Leading Behind the Badge

ABOUT THE AUTHOR

Ronnie Ashmore is the author of several books in the western and police mystery genres. His primary focus is the western genre where his books are packed with realism and grit. A former police officer and two time Chief of Police, he writes with an authority of the places and the people of his stories. When not writing he enjoys playing golf, traveling, and spending time with his family. He can be reached through
social media or by email at

ronnieashmorebooks@gmail.com.

ABOUT THE PUBLISHER

Creative Texts is a boutique independent publishing house devoted to high quality content that readers enjoy. We publish best-selling authors such as Ronnie Ashmore, Jerry D. Young, N.C. Reed, Sean Liscom, Jared McVay, Laurence Dahners, and many more. Our audiobook performers are among the best in the business including Hollywood legends like Barry Corbin and top talent like Christopher Lane, Alyssa Bresnaham, Erin Moon and Graham Hallstead.

Whether its post-apocalyptic or dystopian fiction, biography, history, true crime science fiction, thrillers, or even classic westerns, our goal is to produce highly rated customer preferred content. If there is anything we can do to enhance your reader experience, please contact us directly at info@creativetexts.com. As always, we do appreciate your reviews on your book seller's website.

Finally, if you would like to find more great books like this one, please search for us by name in your favorite search engine or on your bookseller's website to see books by all Creative Texts authors.

Thank you for reading!